CRESTFALLEN

CRESTFALLEN
Solitude

Gabriella Francis

ARCHWAY
PUBLISHING

Archway Publishing books may be ordered through booksellers or by contacting:

Archway Publishing
1663 Liberty Drive
Bloomington, IN 47403
www.archwaypublishing.com
1-(888)-242-5904

Because of the dynamic nature of the Internet, any web addresses or links contained in
this book may have changed since publication and may no longer be valid. The views
expressed in this work are solely those of the author and do not necessarily reflect the
views of the publisher, and the publisher hereby disclaims any responsibility for them.

Any people depicted in stock imagery provided by Thinkstock are models,
and such images are being used for illustrative purposes only.
Certain stock imagery © Thinkstock.

ISBN: 978-1-4808-0396-1 (sc)
ISBN: 978-1-4808-0397-8 (e)

Library of Congress Control Number: 2013920675

Printed in the United States of America

Archway Publishing rev. date: 12/23/2013

This book is dedicated in loving memory of beloved grandfather, Edward Feanny, for always believing in me.

And the angels which kept not their first estate, but left their own habitation, he hath reserved in everlasting chains under darkness unto the judgment of the great day.

—*Jude 1:16*

CONTENTS

PROLOGUE

The grinning moon crested above the rippling black waters of the calm ocean. The lingering scent of salt filled my nose, and the sound of waves lapping against the sand of the shore brought a smile to my face. I always enjoyed staying out late at night, looking out over the serene waters. It put me into a comatose state.

It was the one place where I could just sit, relax, and watch the rippling waves licking the shore, keeping me company.

Strands of my light brown hair fell into my face from the wind, but I brushed them back. I heard the rustling of leaves and branches in the shadowy forest beside the shore, swishing as if whispering to the wind.

I was a curious girl, but curiosity was one thing that attracted danger—and danger was the one thing that was waiting for me tonight.

A strange soaring sound that overpowered the slapping waves brought me to sentience.

I felt a puzzled expression rise on my face as I hastily scanned the vast breadth of seawater beyond the foamy shoreline, searching for what had aroused me. My attention turned to the sky, where I saw a black winged shadow dart across the light of the moon. Two screaming hawks of metal rocketed after it—government fighter jets.

"What the hell?" I shouted, barely aware of the words I was forming.

Sparks of light burst from the jets, and I recognized them for what they were: bullets.

The bullets zipped through the air, clearly trying to hit the winged figure, but the silhouette danced and sliced through the air, dodging the gunfire. Darkness shrouded the night sky, but the moonlight over the ocean provided just enough lighting for me to see the details.

The silhouette fluttered through the air in athletic, rapid, almost graceful motions as it dodged the tearing bullets. Through the soaring noise of the fighter jets, I swore I could distinctly hear the constant, swift flapping of the silhouette's black wings.

In sharp arcs and dives, the silhouette darted around the shower of bullets.

Then, as if hit by a natural instinct, I rapidly searched my pockets for my iPhone. I *had* to get this on video. I let out a small grunt of disappointment when I realized I had left it at home. Finding nothing else to do, I continued to watch the fight with excitement pulsing through my veins.

The silhouette zoomed ceaselessly through the dark air as if a part of the atmosphere itself. It then flew higher into the black heavens, its dark form blending in with the sky and only decipherable by starlight. The jets followed.

The black silhouette vaulted its wings out farther, gaining altitude as it rose and dipped, flying higher and higher.

I didn't know exactly what was happening or what had caused the battle, but whatever it was, it was giving me an adrenaline rush.

The bullets didn't stop whizzing out. Before I could process what happened, the figure began to fall, red liquid flying out in thin lines from one of its wings.

Its wings tilted upward from the pressure of the fall as it plummeted at an angle into the dark forest along the shoreline, kicking branches and leaves up into the air.

I jerked, bringing a hand to my lips, paralyzed by shock. What happened? It was shot down—was it going to die? What exactly was *it*?

I watched as the jets hovered midair a bit before they rocketed out of sight.

Staying where I was, I tried to process what just happened before my eyes. Questions circulated in my thoughts like leaves in a whirlwind. What did I just see? For a curious person, I despised questions. A fight between a strange winged creature and government fighter jets was something you'd see in a movie, not real life. If I hadn't been hallucinating, I wanted to see behind the curtains of the show. This couldn't be over.

Desperate to get the poking and prodding questions out of my thoughts, I sauntered toward the dark forest, my pace slow at first but then frenzied as I ran to see what had fallen. Curiosity killed the cat.

Pine trees towered over me and gray stones loomed above me as I strolled through the dark forest, relying on memory to take me where I last saw the silhouette fall. The outward stretch of the branches blocked out the moonlight, allowing the darkness to invade my vision.

I focused on the dirt pathway below my feet as my only source of direction. My shoes crunching over the dead leaves made me shudder and gave me the unwanted sense that I wasn't alone.

Owls hooted in the distance, mingling with the howling of a pack of wolves. A heavy fog hung in the air, settling over the forest and darkening the trees overhead. The thick scent of maple wood filled my nose, swirling around my lungs with a sweet aroma, but it calmed my racing pulse only slightly.

A black smudge that stood out against the light brown pathway caught my attention. I moved closer and plucked it from where it lay.

A black feather.

It was about the size of my forearm, and the silky black threads reflected gray against what little light the moon offered.

I looked ahead of where I was, noticing more of them

scattered across the ground. The trail led somewhere off the path and into the skulking darkness that seemed to spiral in front of my vision like a black ribbon, tempting me to go in. I followed the trail of black feathers.

As I led myself into the mass of shadows, I felt something hard and prickly slap against my arm.

I jolted and whirled around to see what had touched me, the hairs on the nape of my neck standing on end. I realized it was just a tree branch. Suddenly, I realized that maybe going through the forest—especially alone—wasn't as good an idea as I had thought.

Still, I was questioning and determined. I wanted to know what animal had been shot down from the skies. The feathers were way too big for it to have been any bird that I knew of.

Drops and splatters of red liquid began to fuse with the feathers. The fallen animal had tumbled over the uprooted trees, leaving them painted with blood. Torn tree trunks and bare branches with their leaves ripped out towered over me like skeletons.

I pushed the branches and brushwood out of my way, and my blood froze when I saw what was lying in the center of the clearing.

A dark angel.

His black wings were missing half of the feathers that they seemed to require. The wingspan had to be at least as long as my full-size bed. His arm was bent at a painful angle, and his frail yet muscular body lay sprawled facedown in a pool of blood. The shadowy trees and bushes formed an uneven circle around his motionless form. He seemed to be unconscious.

If the situation hadn't been so grave, I would've blushed at the fact that he wasn't wearing anything.

I froze where I stood, unsure whether I should run away or stay longer to get a closer look at what was going on. *Ha,* I thought, *look at that.* A real angel lying right there, and there I was, gawking at him with no camera. No proof.

Just like always, curiosity took control of my actions, and I dared a step closer. When the angel didn't move, I took another. The angel's right arm made a sudden jolt, and I froze in my tracks, setting the hazard limits. Danger seemed to roll off him like a heavy scent.

The angel slowly opened his eyes, and the first place he directed them was to the black sky. I broke the limits I had set and stepped closer.

We were separated by a few feet when the angel made an attempt at standing up. He only got onto his knees before his hands slipped on the blood-soaked grass and he faltered. Trembling, he rolled over to his back and lay there, staring at the sky as if expecting a black hole to open and pull him into its darkness.

I didn't realize that I was closing the space between us at a much faster pace until the angel turned his head my way, a dangerous smile surfacing on his face.

I didn't move. I couldn't. The way he held my gaze paralyzed me from the inside out.

We stood there, each of us staring at the other's face and

not moving a muscle. My breath was visible in the air—swirling beyond my vision and catching the moonlight before materializing back into nothing.

Slowly, I tilted my head to the side in question. *Who are you?*

The angel smiled, but the emotion burning behind his eyes was anything but serenity. "Jared."

I blinked in surprise. Why did he say that? Was that his name? The uneasy thought that he could read my mind chilled me to the bone. I'd heard that angels could read your emotions, but seeing it in reality produced a layer of goose bumps on my skin.

I stepped closer, my heart leaping up into my throat when I saw two gashes from the bullets deep in his right wing. Trickles of blood ran along his black feathers. Even so, Jared didn't seem to care. It was as if he couldn't feel it. All his attention was focused on me.

I risked a question, wondering if he could understand. "Why were those government jets chasing you?"

Jared remained totally still except for the unbroken rise and fall of his chest. "I let my guard down."

Since I didn't know exactly what that answer meant, I sought another. "Are you a real dark angel?"

His smile grew wider. "I don't look like one?"

Before I could open my mouth to say something else, a vibrant light shifted my attention to the left. A spotlight from the sky shone through the thick branches, and the sound of helicopter blades slicing the air rang in my ears.

Jared's dark smile vanished from his face and an expression of alarm replaced it. Instinctively, he rolled over to his hands and knees once more, trying again to get up. Loose ends of his long, black hair fell over his ashen eyes.

Acting on impulse, I dropped to his side, hooked his arm over my neck, and pulled him into a standing position. Even for the sheer size of his wings, he was surprisingly light; it was as though I was holding the weight of a large fabric replica on my shoulder.

The helicopter engine grew louder, encouraging me to get out of there.

It suddenly occurred to me that carrying a dark angel out of government property wasn't such a good idea. I mean, seriously? Saving a *dark* angel? But there was something about him—something that told me to never judge a book by its cover.

Again relying on memory, I navigated our way out of the forest, hastily working through the thicket of trees and bushes and back to where I had been earlier—which wasn't a good thing. The clear sky gave the jets and helicopters a better chance to spot us, and that was something I definitely did not want to risk.

With the thought spinning circles in my head, I quickened my steps, and we rapidly moved toward my car.

Our feet sank into the sand, slowing our pace and giving gave me a fresh rush of panic. I could feel the government aircrafts approaching. I knew they had spotted me running with Jared, and it didn't exactly put a warm feeling inside me.

I peered ahead and made out the outline of my blue Passat at the edge of the parking lot. I reached out to grab the door handle before I was even close enough to grasp it.

I yanked the handle, but the door didn't budge.

Locked.

I swore under my breath and hastily slapped my pockets in search of my car keys. *Please don't tell me I dropped them in the forest. Please don't tell me I dropped them in the forest.*

I felt the familiar lump of my car keys in my back pocket and pinched them out. My fingers fumbled with the buttons as I unlocked the car. I had just flung the door open and helped Jared into the passenger seat when a pulsating light swept over the car.

I looked up, bringing my hand to my eyes to block out the blinding light of the government copter.

On instinct, I threw myself into the driver seat, stuck the keys into the ignition, and stomped on the gas, not even waiting for the engine to warm up.

The wheels buffed the road, and the vehicle swerved before it drove off.

I couldn't see the spotlight anymore, but that didn't give me a reason to believe that the aircraft had stopped chasing me. I yanked the wheel to the left, rounding a turn in hopes of shaking them off, but to no avail.

I didn't keep the Passat at a steady pace, knowing that if I drove straight, I would run the risk of the pilots inside the aircraft seeing my license plate clearly. I wondered what they were thinking of me now—drunk driving, probably.

I was too busy gluing my eyes to the street to look at Jared. When I did, I felt my heart skip a beat.

His wings were gone.

He noticed me staring and shrugged as if nothing was going on, giving me a look that said, *I'll explain later.*

I grunted and leaned closer to the windshield, trying to view above the car to make sure the helicopters were gone. The sharp clanging sound to my left and right told me otherwise.

Great. Now they were trying to shoot me. What had I gotten myself into?

Up ahead, I noticed a thicket of trees that blocked out all view from the sky. Frantically, I set my direction there.

Once the thick branches' shadows were blanketing the Passat, I stomped the brake, heaving the car to a complete stop. The echo of my screeching tires faded into the distance.

My breathing was heavy, and black stained the edges of my vision. My hands refused to let go of the wheel. In the thick darkness outside the car, I was barely able to see the slow-moving spotlight seeping through the tree branches, searching for us. I turned to Jared, trying to regain a normal heartbeat. "I think you owe me an explanation."

Jared threw off a dangerous grin. "Hmm. Where to start ..."

I was shocked at his ability to be chased down by the government and still look tranquil. I was beginning to wonder.

"How long were you being chased down?"

"Months." He said it so naturally, so insouciantly, I almost didn't believe him. "Maybe there was a reason I fell next to you. Maybe it was destiny." His smile grew wider. "Like your name."

I didn't want to know how he knew my name.

He continued, "You see, the reason you could see my wings before and can't now is because I can control when people can see them."

I pondered this. "If you can control when people can see your wings, why didn't you just stop the pilots from seeing them?"

"There was too much technology in the way for me to touch their minds."

I stared at him.

"I can only interact with humans' thoughts through clear channels. If there's too much machinery in the way, I can't really do anything." His flirty smile gradually became grave while he said this. He was finally taking notice of the situation.

Jared gave me a look that told me we were done talking.

"I still have questions," I said quickly, trying unsuccessfully to catch his attention before it shifted to the copters that were still circling overhead.

"Some questions can't get answers."

I followed his gaze and swallowed around the lump in my throat. My next question was the most concerning. "What am I going to do?"

Without warning, he opened the car door.

"What are you doing?" I shrieked in a tiny voice to avoid unwanted attention.

"I'm going to draw them off while you run." His expression was soft but serious.

I suddenly felt a small shred of compassion that quickly multiplied into dread.

"What about your wings? Aren't you injured?"

In response, his wings suddenly burst from his back like explosives. I saw that the bullet wounds were completely healed, despite small streaks of dried blood in his feathers. *Okay, instant healing,* I thought. *That's one new thing I learned about dark angels.*

Still, in my mind I replayed the moment when I saw him being shot down from the sky—that dreadful, tense scene when I saw him lying seemingly lifeless in the middle of the forest, surrounded by his own blood. Looking at the government copters drained away all remaining hope.

I could sense Jared taking notice of my concern. He leaned back into the car, took my face in his hands, and kissed me in caring, fond affection.

All the troubles and problems that surrounded me seemed to slither from my grip like sand. It was like gravity had decided to abandon me.

I recalled the times in my life when I'd been kissed, but none could compare to the way he did it. I inhaled the strong scent of earth and spice.

As his lips parted from mine, it felt like the weight of a truck had been dropped on me.

I watched as Jared climbed out of the Passat, stretching out his mighty black wings. With his back to me, he said, "Once I get their full attention, drive away." His wings slapped the air, and he zoomed into the black sky.

Once I saw the aircraft chase Jared farther and farther into the night, I lazily set the gear into drive and steered my way back home. I faintly heard the resonating echo of gunfire and the flapping of wings. Jared's presence hadn't left me. He had saved my life.

An angel of darkness had saved my life.

Chapter 1

REAPPEARANCE

I decided not to tell anybody about what had happened that night. Hundreds of reasons why I shouldn't crowded together.

First of all, if I told one of my friends about it, then word would get out, and risking having the government know about what I saw was the last thing I wanted to do. Second, if I told my dad, I knew he would go to the government in the blink of an eye.

You see, my dad wasn't one of those parents who showed affection. If I didn't cook him dinner, I'd have to go without food for a week. Whenever he got bored, he would leisurely produce his leather belt. I couldn't even remember the last time he said the words "I love you."

Abusive dads made no sense at all, in my opinion.

My dad barely allowed me to go out with my friends. He limited my TV time to a half hour a day (sometimes not letting me use it at all) and never let me go to the skate park. His favorite hobbies were drinking, sleeping, and beating me whenever something didn't go his way.

This morning (just like every morning), I had to fix his bed as soon as he got up, make him breakfast exactly the way he wanted it, and skip brushing my hair to make time for doing his "chores." An invisible hand clutched my heart in a tight, cold grip.

My mom, on the other hand ... she used to be *so* nice to me. She would let me stay out late at the theaters, let me stay over at a friend's house, and even allowed me to watch *Family Guy*. When my dad had an itchy, punch-your-daughter fist, she would always stand between us and stop the situation before it could get too out of hand. But all that changed the day she died. I never wished as much as I did on that day that they had a cure for cancer.

My dad took advantage of her death. He took her place in the house—in my life—and used me as his personal punching bag.

Behind the houses, nestled on the higher ground beside the sidewalk, tall pine trees stood against the hazy, early morning skyline, looking as if they were set aflame by the piercing sun.

It was late August. School had just begun and—unlike for some other kids—this was good news for me. It meant I got a full seven hours away from home.

I wasn't really one of those girls who loved to go to the

mall and go shoe shopping. I was more like a rocker girl who listened to heavy metal instead of falling in love with Justin Bieber or One Direction. And I could act a little immature for my age—seventeen—especially outside of school.

But that night had changed everything.

I replayed the moment when Jared kissed me—that passionate second when his lips made contact with mine, the silent heat rippling through me, the way his touch ignited flames to the ice that froze my bones in place, warming my skin.

I touched my lips. It still felt like his mouth was pressed to mine.

Still caught in the moment, I closed my eyes and altered the reality. I imagined myself tracing my hands along his jawline. He softly stroked his thumbs over my cheekbones in a slow, circular motion, melting my stone-cold core and finishing the touch with a tilt of my chin, my eyes facing his ...

Realizing I had nearly stepped right into a busy road, I shoved the thoughts and memories aside, focusing on the job at hand.

Not wanting to be seen in the same car the government aircraft had seen me with, I decided to walk to school and put up with the crisp, frosty morning air that numbed the tip of my nose. I would keep the Passat locked up in the garage for a few months, and once the coast was clear, I would get back in the driver seat and cruise the open roads.

The barbed-wire fences and dewy blades of grass created no distraction from what was spinning around in my head. I wondered what had happened to Jared. Did he escape the fighter jets and choppers? I hoped so. But if he had, where was he?

I sighed, creating a cloud of vapor in the air, and slung my bag higher on my shoulder. The thought of going to school after what had happened last night seemed almost ludicrous. Here I was, walking to school right after being chased down by the government, as if everything was fine, and I couldn't tell anyone about it. I couldn't believe this.

But I would stay glued to the lies that were forming into excuses, just to stay safe. Better to be circled by deceit than to be surrounded by certain death.

My feet were beginning to hurt, so I reeled my head up to the gray sky to cause a distraction. The sky was vacant, except for a few isolated, dark clouds. Up ahead, I could see the sun's rays slicing through the parting clouds, telling me to hurry up and get to class before it was too late. I ignored the thought, knowing that I could never get to school on time at this pace. I didn't even have an admit form to excuse me.

I imagined entering the attendance office with a note from the government: "Please excuse Destiny Aubrey for entering school late today. She was being chased down by military aircraft while running away with the dark angel we've been searching for."

A smile of dry amusement formed on my face.

A familiar car slowed to a stop next to me, and I stared at the person who sat behind the wheel.

"Hey," Crystal said as soon as she lowered the passenger

side window, bobbing her head in time with the music blasting from the speakers. "Need a ride?"

All pressure weighing on me dissipated. "Thanks, Crystal," I said as I clicked open the door and slumped in the seat, completely out of breath. "I don't know what I'd do without you."

Crystal had been my best friend since kindergarten. She was one of the few reasons I smiled in my solitary life. The moment I met her, she seemed to fill in the blanks to give me a purpose. She was also the kind of girl who liked listening to heavy metal, like Black Veil Brides or Metallica, and she always seemed to have her radio turned on full blast.

I slightly envied her ability to keep her hair perfectly straight despite how hard she rocked her head to the racing music. It seemed that no matter how much advice she gave me to keep my hair straightened and still dance like I was drunk, I never could maintain perfect hair at a school dance.

Crystal reached for her purse under the seat and produced a pink hairbrush, which I used to untangle the knots that had formed on the nape of my neck. I cursed my dad for asking for such a stupid breakfast that I had to make from scratch. I could've been late for school!

We decided to ignore the speed limit—which we were ten miles over—and sing along with Skillet's covers.

"Ooh, I finally got my hands on that song you were asking for last week!" Crystal shouted over the thrashing music.

"Which one?" I yelled back, remembering my music requests.

"Seether feat. Amy Lee's 'Broken'!" she replied, immediately changing the music and setting it to a higher volume. She grunted her disappointment when she realized it couldn't go any higher.

I squealed at the first few lyrics that came out and lashed my hands in the air in a rock symbol and head banging in rhythm with the song.

We always silently laughed at the people who never knew any of the music we listened to. We couldn't care less, anyway.

When we pulled into the school parking lot, we remained in the car for a few more minutes to savor the last of the music we could listen to before we went to class.

Crystal checked the time on her phone. "Crap! We've only got three minutes!"

I froze at what I heard. "So then what are we *doing*? Let's *go*!" I snatched my backpack from the backseat and threw myself out of the car. I ran in a frenzy to the entrance of the school gates, which—thank goodness—were still open.

The faint *thump, thump, thump* of music still lingered in the back of my head.

I was glad I bumped into Crystal on my way to school. She always seemed to flush away all the worries and stress that poked and prodded me with her hilarious attitude and ability to make people laugh no matter their mood.

Half the courtyard was empty by the time we got into the school. High school students were packed at the building doors, making it seemingly impossible to get through in one piece.

Despite all the commotion, I caught something out of the corner of my eye that put a weight in my stomach. His eyes seemed to slice through all the distraction, burning straight into mine.

Jared was leaning against the wall of the tall stadium that stood at the edge of the courtyard. Unlike the last time I saw him, he was wearing a black T-shirt with dark blue skinny jeans. His black wings were visible, but no one seemed to notice. He was probably toying with the students' minds, not allowing them to see his wings.

The thought of getting to class on time walked out the door. I almost dropped my backpack in shock (and relief) and ran to him in desire, not even thinking about hiding my concern.

The school bell rang as I threw my arms around him. "You're okay!" I said.

I could almost feel his lips take on a devilish curve with his flirtatious quip. "You *make* me okay."

A thought struck me that made me stare at my feet and allowed me to sink deep into thought. Wasn't he a dark angel? Last time I checked, most dark angels were described as soulless, cold, and mostly narcissistic. Why was he revealing emotion to me?

I looked into his gray eyes, searching for something that might bring me close to an answer.

"How did you escape?" I asked quickly, distress in my voice.

He nodded to me with an almost casual flick of his head. "You."

Could he say anything longer than six words?

Caught off guard, I felt myself give off a frisky smile. "Thinking of me gets you away from government pursuits." My tone sounded doubtful, despite the sarcasm. I hadn't forgotten about our little kiss. "I'll answer that for myself. You got away for what probably is the hundredth time because you're immortal. You can live forever."

"Without you, forever won't be too long." His voice was like black silk that passionately caressed my soul.

I knew most girls would run away from the first dark angel they saw, but I was undeniably different. If you had an abusive father who didn't give a shit about your existence, you'd rather go and date some dark angel who saved you from being taken by the government.

He leaned back against the wall. "So."

I gave him a look of disbelief and eagerness. "So what?"

You said you wanted questions.

I blinked. "How did you do that?"

His expression was engraved with doubt, like he didn't know what I was talking about. He was doing a crummy act. "Do what?"

"You know what."

"Well, there's your first question."

"Can I get an answer?"

"Maybe."

Maybe? What kind of response was that? Anyway, I had my answer. Jared had told me last night that he could touch human's thoughts through clear channels. I had no doubt that involved speaking through their minds.

Jared uttered a playful laugh that made me feel warm and slippery inside. "So, first question."

I took advantage of the moment. "How does this—thing—work? How can you read people's minds and make them see things?" I shivered; the moment when I heard his voice speaking in my mind still lingered. It felt like his voice zoned out all other words circulating in my thoughts.

"Deceiving?" Jared corrected in a questioning tone. "All immortals can do it, and it's kind of easy. You just literally think of something—a sentence, an image, a memory—and then will yourself to push it forth to the other person."

Like this, he deceived. An image of pure red and white roses was produced out of thin air and locked into my hands. The details of the flowers seemed so realistic, so graphic; I was almost tempted to believe they were real. I didn't resist the urge to raise the roses to my face, breathing in the sweet, honey-like scent that lingered with an alluring, evocative aroma.

I jerked when a thorn pricked my finger. The roses materialized out of my hands, leaving them empty. I remembered I still had way too many questions.

Seeing the intent look tattooing his face, I continued with the previous discussion, hoping to keep his attention. "Why were those government fighter jets shooting you?"

"If they see a dark angel flying in the sky, they're not going to just leave it alone."

"Where are you from?"

"Next question."

I remained silent.

Jared ran his fingers through my hair in an affectionate motion, but his eyes, sharp and grave, seemed to pierce straight through mine. I realized I had pushed the wrong button. "Look, there's a lot that you don't know about me, and it's better off staying that way. A lot of people with dark pasts aren't really the ones who find it fun to share."

I made a soft noise that was torn between a laugh and a grunt. "Do you really think you're alone?"

It didn't really take him long to figure out what I was saying—either because he had intelligence far stronger than any mortal, or because he could just read my mind.

All solemnity seemed to leave his eyes, and his caress moved from my hair to my face. His thumbs smoothly stroked my cheekbones. A sharp sigh escaped me.

I glanced into Jared's eyes before closing my own, feeling my joints melt away. So close to his warm chest, I could hear his heart beating with a steady thumping rhythm.

Jared wrapped his black, velvety wings around me, blocking out all the cold air that stung my skin.

Something was fluttering in my chest. Every time I gave Jared's eyes a glance, all pain and conflict around me seemed to crumble, as if made of sand. The memories of my dad's torment didn't seem as powerful. Instead, they grew vague.

I was addicted to Jared like a drug. His touch alone seemed to whisk away all the troubles and fights back at home, which was something I'd needed for a long time. Looking at him was like staring at an incomplete painting, Jared the only color contrasting against the pale canvas.

He smelled of soap, earth, and herbs, so enticing, so alluring. The memories of last night came rushing back in a wave of passion.

He slowly pulled me in for a second kiss, holding my waist. His mouth lightly brushed against mine—and then the ringing of the tardy bell screamed in my ears.

I swore and pulled away. "I have to get to class or my teacher is going to kill me! I don't even have an admit!" Panic rose and boiled in my chest. Worse than the teachers was my dad. If word got to him that I was late ... I shuddered at the thought.

Jared read my thoughts—literally. "I can get you in class without an admit."

"How?" I asked. I knew he could read minds and make people hallucinate, but was he really going to deceive my teacher? If so—awesome.

"Just walk in the room. The teacher won't ask you for an admit once you get in. No one will." With a flick of his head, he gestured to my building. I followed his gaze and wondered what he was going to do.

When I turned back, he was gone.

I WAS USED TO HEARING the bell ring when I got into class. Entering this time seemed foreign enough. Just like Jared said, once I walked in, the teacher didn't even take notice of me. It was as if I didn't exist.

My first-period class consisted of seven rows of six chairs and a faint trace of Gucci Guilty perfume that unquestionably belonged to Jade.

Her conceited sneer immediately made me grind my teeth in rage, and her gelled curly hair with blonde dyed at the tips didn't exactly lighten my mood. Her light brown eyes made it so easy to fool people into thinking of her as innocent. No, those eyes were pure evil in guiltless garb.

Jade was a spitting image of my dad's personality—she enjoyed intimidating me and savoring each and every moment. She was always there. From the moment I stepped into kindergarten to this very day, she'd spread rumors, spawned gangs around me, and even shoved me into the wall whenever I saw her in the hallway.

And the worst part? She sat right next to me in first period. What a great way to start your day, huh?

I strolled absentmindedly to my desk, trying not to make eye contact. Nonetheless, Jade beamed cruelly at me, pure malice lacing her features.

I let my backpack fall from my shoulders and land soundlessly on the floor, slumped in my seat, and turned away from my archenemy, trying to block out the first words that escaped her lips.

"Ugh. No, no, no. This can't be happening. Do I really have to sit next to *Medusa*?"

She thought that just because my hair got a little kinky, she had the right to call me Greek monsters' names. The way she spoke to me, it was as if she had authority over my life.

"You sit next to me every day. What do you want this time?"

"What I want is for you to get that nasty hair out of my face. Have you ever heard of Herbal Essences shampoo?"

I would've had time to fix my hair this morning if it hadn't been for my dad—though I had already decided not to tell anyone about his abuse. There were too many memories in my house of my mom, and I didn't want to be sent to a foster home and have them give away the house.

I had managed to collect enough information to know that Jade didn't feel the same pain I did. In fact, she lived the richest, happiest life and didn't have mean parents. But she was abusing her advantage.

They say that if you are getting bullied, you should go tell a guidance counselor—but no. That never worked for me.

It seemed that whenever I reported anything she'd done to me, nothing happened. She would either find a way to turn the blame around on me, or the staff members would become too lazy to help. Tell an adult, my ass.

I had a special comeback for her insult climbing up my throat, but I held it back. The last thing I wanted was to get myself locked away in the detention room with her. The last time *that* happened, I made up an excuse to use the bathroom, locked myself in one of the stalls, and listened to my solitary sobs echoing off the walls.

Keep talking. One day you'll say something smart, I screamed in my head. It was the only place I had privacy.

Or so I thought.

Watch what happens to her grades at the end of the school year. Which class do you want her to flunk first? I heard Jared's voice in the back of my mind.

I couldn't snag the smile that curved on my face.

Chapter 2

EXPOSURE

As the dismissal bell rang, I instinctively got up from my desk and headed out the door, almost forgetting my book bag.

The last thing I wanted was to have my biology team keep me in class for another hour. They would do this *every* day I had biology—keep the whole group locked up inside the classroom, talking about card games or anime instead of discussing any upcoming assignments or studying for the next test.

I learned the hard way to always—*always*—walk out the door as soon as the bell rang and pretend that I didn't hear my team calling after me.

I slung my bag over my shoulder and started walking toward the parking lot, but I then remembered that I had left my Passat locked inside the garage to avoid suspicion. I would have to start walking home from now on.

But if I kept doing that, wouldn't my dad question me?

My dad always wanted to know exactly what I'd been doing, why I'd been doing it, and who I hung out with. If I didn't tell him, he had the chance to use his metal-laced leather belt. There seemed to be no other reason for why I barely went out on the weekends. I always had to "stay at home," "do your chores," or "stop being lazy."

There was only one thing that kept me going forward: my dad leaving for work for the entire week.

Since it was Friday, I would only have to endure one more day with him before he would have to leave. I smiled at what I could do while he was gone—what I could do with Jared.

My walking pace seemed to lag and cast away the rapidly running footsteps of excited high school students fighting to reach the front gates first. While the students around me were focused solely on getting out of school, my thoughts centered on the one person who melted my heart.

Jared had told me earlier to meet him out in the courtyard, and that set off my questions for what he had planned.

By the time I had rounded a few turns, jogged down a hallway, and shoved open the double doors, my heart skipped a beat.

Jared leaned against the one of the circular stone pillars supporting the tin roof that sheltered the walkway. Like last time, no one noticed him—or his black wings. Students filed around him as they continued with their day, a few of them walking straight through his wings. The edges of his mouth tipped upward in a mischievous, flirty smile.

He spoke into my mind. *Come on, Cupid. I'll save you from the horror of school.*

I felt myself smirk.

Cupid.

The idea of it being too early for pet names lodged itself in my thoughts, but I quickly flushed it away. Despite Jared being a dark angel, I felt connected to him by a magnetic pull that I would probably never understand, let alone neglect. The way he spoke to me—something about it screamed to me that he was trying to defend me.

I followed Jared to the backside of the school grounds, where rusty fences outlined the area and puddles of water and oil dotted the gravel. There had been reports of student disappearances in this section of the school campus.

No one ever visited this part of the school, and its appearance seemed to scream *empty*. This triggered my confusion.

Jared must've noticed my concern, because he threw me a reassuring smile. "Relax. We just need to be in a place where no other humans can see us."

This didn't lower my guard.

All the affection that had once churned off him suddenly dissolved. I took a step back, keeping my distance in case I had to run.

Jared's solid expression eased, and he tried striding closer, only making me move back. *You don't trust me yet.*

All instinct inside of me was begging and screaming at me

to run away. *You're an angel in black. You're being chased by the government. You took me to the back of the school, where no one else will ever see us. In my world, it's kind of hard to trust someone with all these features.*

What was I thinking? Falling in love with a dark angel was something you'd see in a movie or a romance novel and had nothing to do with reality. I had an abusive dad, but I had found someone who could possibly drown out the pain, making me numb to him. I had two options—dangerous pleasure and distinctive pain. But which was worth it?

Jared took another step toward me. I tried stepping back, but my back hit a wall.

Jared's hand found its way to my face, and he caressed my cheekbone. I squeezed my eyes shut. I flinched, ready for anything, but Jared remained deathly still. I heard him sigh. *What can I do to make you trust me, to make you love me the same way I love you?*

If he thought he could reach my heart with Shakespeare bullshit, he was wrong.

Cupid.

I looked up at him, and the look in his eyes attempted to shatter my uncertainty. I was torn between love and hate, each side pulling my arms in need.

Jared's finger tilted my chin up, allowing me to read his eyes. *Please. Let me earn your trust.*

I sighed, knowing that I had to say something. I felt myself swaying, and my eyes burned with tears. I wouldn't cry in front of him.

"I want you to answer my questions." I pushed determination into my voice, hoping he wouldn't recognize my fear. I was doing a lousy job at it. "If you think reading my thoughts unnoticed and allowing me to fall in love with you without knowing a thing about your past is okay, then you're wrong."

I knew my dad, and I knew ways around the pain he caused me. But I had just met Jared—a dark angel. How was I supposed to know whether he would cause an agonizing betrayal later on? Did he do that with other girls as well?

Jared didn't move. His eyes seemed to take on a faraway look that defined his depth in thought.

"Jared."

The sound of my voice made him instinctively straighten.

"Why are you an angel of darkness?" I would start there. I knew he *had* to be someone good before he had gone rogue, but who was he back then? Why had his wings turned black?

He closed his eyes, rested his hands on the back of his neck, and bowed his head as if waiting to fall into death. I noticed he was trying to ignore my question.

"Jared." The sheer command in my tone snapped his attention back to reality once more.

Jared stared at me with his own black power. "Cupid, the consequences—"

"Do you want me to trust you or not?" I said, cutting off anything else he had to say. If he wanted to earn my trust, this was the only way he could, whether he liked it or not.

Jared blinked, and he moved his hands to my face once more. His closing expression told me he had come to a decision.

"I'm going to warn you. Be prepared for what I'm going to show you. Leave your comfort zone before you watch it."

I nodded, wondering what he meant by "before you watch it." What was he going to do?

Jared bowed his head over me, and his forehead had barely touched mine when a flash of light exploded in the corner of my vision.

I was unconscious before I knew it.

I BLINKED AND SCANNED MY surroundings. An ethereal white haze clouded my vision like a heavy fog hanging in the air. I realized I was looking through Jared's memory, living inside his past.

I was lying in the middle of a black alleyway, the dark clouds up ahead draping the moon from view. Directly across the street, flashing neon lights and thumping music emanated from bars and clubs. I looked to the dead-end side of the alley and saw a girl about my age pressed against the brick wall in fear.

Shielding most of her body from my sight was a man who looked to be about in his midtwenties. In his right hand, he clutched a wallet, and in his left, he held a pistol.

Though the scene itself was shocking, I was distracted by something entirely different: Jared.

He was standing behind the man clearly horrified at the scene, but something about him was different. His wings were ... white.

He was a guardian angel.

The girl's guardian angel, I quickly noted.

But neither of them seemed to notice me or Jared.

The man rummaged through the wallet, hastily counting the money inside of it. He shook his head. "This isn't all you have." He looked back up at the girl, making her flinch. "I know you have more."

Tears rolled down the girl's face, and her eyes never wavered from the gun. "I don't have any more!" she screamed, every corner of the alley echoing her voice, amplifying her fear.

The man tilted back the hammer of the pistol. "You're trying my patience."

The girl threw her arms over her head to shield herself from the inevitable. "Please! Leave me alone!"

The resulting sound of the gunshot made me jump, and I was paralyzed in astonishment.

The girl was violently flung against the wall from the force of the bullet. Blood painted the bricks, and the hole from the bullet was clearly visible through her eye.

Her body dropped lifelessly to the floor, and the man sauntered to it and began rapidly searching her pockets, glancing frequently at the street to make sure no unwanted eyes witnessed what was happening.

I held Jared's gaze, now locked on the scene in dread and silent shock.

Why was I being shown this? Was this how Jared became dark? Were his human's actions the cause of—?

No. The human had nothing to do with his actions. I knew a guardian angel's job was solely to protect and guard humans. So what happened?

My questions were answered when I saw Jared's facial features automatically harden.

I watched as he grabbed the back of the man's neck. The man froze, and the thought of what Jared was going to do wouldn't find its way into my thoughts—and I didn't want it to.

The man—by himself—buried the barrel of the gun in his mouth and squeezed the trigger.

Blood showered the ground and walls, giving the graffiti a more violent appearance. A sickening feeling crawled up in my stomach. I wondered if I would vomit inside the vision or in real life.

Jared removed his hand from the man's neck, allowing him to fall lifelessly to the ground. A fusion of regret and liberation brimmed behind his eyes, and a tint of blackness slowly crawled through his wings' white feathers.

My breathing was heavy, and my entire body trembled with fright and panic. I looked up to see Jared sulking over me, and I realized we were sitting on the ground. He was pulling me against him.

"I didn't know what else to do. I let my anger find action, and I convinced my human to shoot himself. I regret what I did that night, and it traumatized me for life. As a result, my wings turned black." Jared's eyes were sincere, and his voice quavered with emotion.

The vision seemed grave, but making Jared's wings turn black because he killed someone who deserved to be dead was just plain ludicrous. Even so, Jared had revealed a crucial piece of his past, knotting our trust together a bit more.

"You didn't deserve that."

"Cupid," Jared said, drawing my head against his chest, pulling me closer, "when I first saw you, I knew better than to think I could fall in love with you. But the more I looked at you, the more I came to notice that I could've been wrong. You've changed me from who I was and saved me from myself. What happened with my human—I didn't want it to happen to you. I used to fly around the world, unnoticed, and cause mischief for other people. I wanted to make them feel the pain that I've caused for myself.

"But I was reckless. I started attracting government attention, and I soon spent years on the run, trying to escape my penalty. No one knows my name, and they don't have a clear view of my face, but they know that there's something out there."

But let's have a little fun while we still can. You were out cold for an hour, and I don't think that's a small amount of time taken from what I had planned.

"What *did* you have planned for us?"

Jared scooped me into his arms, and his lips brushed my earlobe. "This."

Without warning, Jared's black wings burst from his back and struck the air, and we were in the skies in a matter of seconds.

Chapter 3

SHADOW

The wind whistled past my ears, and my hair blew back in the breeze. I'd have expected the air to be freezing cold from the sheer height. When I went flying with Jared, on the other hand, the temperature was perfectly fine— either because he tricked me into thinking the air was warm or because fate was being nice to me.

Jared held me tightly in his arms, and I clung onto his neck, my teeth clattering in uncontrollable fear. I wasn't afraid of heights, but I was afraid of Jared loosening his grip on me and letting me fall ...

I knew he wouldn't do it, but I had my safety measures.

Jared's wings repeatedly collided with the air, catching the wind and gaining altitude with each stroke.

He gazed down at me with compassionate eyes. *Trust me yet?*

I stared at him in disbelief. *"This is a dangerous way to bond with someone!"* I had to scream at the top of my lungs for him to hear my voice over the soaring winds.

A playful smile tugged at his mouth. *Speak with me through your mind. It's kind of useless to talk vocally with me up here.*

I uttered a groan, unsure if he could hear it through my voice or my mind. *I really wish you wouldn't just barge into my subconscious like that. I feel like I have no privacy at all.*

Stop worrying, Cupid. I only go in there when I need to.

Tell me more about how it works. I was still a bit shaken by what I'd just seen. Had I *literally* looked into Jared's memory, or was there more to it? *You can make me hallucinate and see things by sending a mental image, but what exactly did you do when you showed me your memory?*

You didn't exactly see into my memory. Actually, I planted moving images—a video—of what I remembered inside your subconscious.

It was then that things started to get confusing. I changed the subject, despite my desire to know more.

So this is your idea of gaining my trust, I thought, dismayed, looking down at the buildings towering below us.

If I don't drop you, it means you can trust me, Jared thought. A small smirk played on his lips, but his eyes were filling themselves to the brim with "Trust me."

Oh, joy.

Isn't it hard to fly with your body's enormous weight? A just-kidding smirk played on my face.

Jared's wings slowed down and moved almost gracefully. *My bones are hollow, so flight is easier for me.*

Large white lumps brushed past my face, leaving me and Jared sprinkled with vapor. He noticed I was staring at the faraway ground and gazed at me with eyes of pure passion and care. *Cupid, look at me.*

Anything was better than looking down.

Despite the screaming winds, I could hear my heart pounding against my ribs. One look at Jared and I almost forgot where I was. I felt like I was living a nightmare wearing a dream's mask.

My brain stopped working for a fraction of a second, but I quickly regained my awareness.

Jared was a dark angel, all right, but there was something about him—something that I couldn't name, something that told me he had been forced down the wrong path.

The flashback had been vivid enough, but I wanted to know more. He said he wanted me to trust him, and I soon found myself sinking into his wish.

Jared's speed had slackened, and his eyes darkened with compassion. Slowly, he leaned his head over me, his eyes watching mine. I felt his teeth graze my ear, and I couldn't help but nuzzle my head in the curve of his shoulder.

His lips moved to my forehead, where he pressed an extended kiss that warmed my skin. I longed for his mouth to move down just a few inches so that his lips touched mine.

Nothing in my life seemed important anymore. All I wanted was Jared. If he was the only thing filling my empty life, there wouldn't be any missing pieces. I didn't care about school, home, or friends. All I wanted was him.

Slowly but eagerly, I tilted my head up. Jared lowered his. Our lips barely touched when an alarming sensation bubbled up in my chest.

In the corner of my vision, I saw a shadow dart through the air at speeds faster than Jared's. I didn't have time to shout out a warning before I was torn from Jared's arms—and fell.

The wind screeched in my ears, and my heart plummeted, so much like my body.

I screamed, through both voice and thought.

My arms and legs flailed in the air, trying uncontrollably to slow my fall. I stretched my arms out, reaching for Jared, who was flying down after me. I saw the silhouette follow, and I had a split-second clear view of what it was.

It had the black body of a human and the wings of a dragon, which were three times the size of its form. Though it lacked detail, one look at it made me want to vomit. The entire figure resembled a 3-D shadow.

I screamed once more and felt Jared's hands on my fingers. His hands locked a grip on mine, but the silhouette plowed into me, once again knocking me out of Jared's reach. Pain spiked down my arm, but I reached for Jared again.

I couldn't see the silhouette, but I knew it was near.

I heard Jared's voice in my thoughts. *It's okay, Cupid. I'll save you.*

I was fearful of what would happen if he didn't. I could almost feel the ground rushing up to meet me. I focused all my attention on Jared. His wings were outstretched to gain speed, and his arms extended toward me. Worry and panic boiled in his eyes, mirroring mine.

Again, I felt Jared's hands grip my fingers, but the silhouette knocked me from his grip again. I tumbled through the air at an angle, nonstop. I tried spreading out my arms to straighten myself, but the world around me spun. I wasn't sure whether I was upside down, but when I looked up, my heart freefell nauseatingly.

Jared had left me.

I frantically searched the skies but saw no sign of him. I should've known better than to trust him. He allowed that ... *thing* to rip me from his tight embrace, let me fall to my death, and abandoned me.

Tears were on the brink of blinding my vision when I saw the silhouette race toward me.

Another shadow darted below me and caught me in midfall.

Jared held me tighter than before as though afraid that I'd slither from his arms like smoke. Despite what was going on around us, I felt a small trace of regret that fumed itself up to dread. I underestimated Jared. I thought he'd left me to fall to my death.

I threw my arms around his neck and buried my face in his shirt. I didn't want to cry, but I could feel the tears burning in my throat. I held them back.

I felt us hover a few feet above the ground before Jared

relaxed his wings and we were back on solid earth. He'd landed somewhere behind a building towering above an empty street, but I knew exactly where I was.

I looked up at him, expecting him to gaze back at me, but his attention was focused on something entirely different: the silhouette was still following us.

Go home and stay there while I draw him off.

Before I could say anything else, Jared was in the skies, leading the silhouette away from me.

That was the second time he'd done that.

I WANTED TO KICK THE front door open, but instead, I locked up my true emotions and used the key. My hand was trembling so much that I could barely fit the key in the keyhole. I couldn't believe what had just happened—and how it all could have happened in less than two days.

The door swung outward. I let my book bag drop from my shoulder as I slammed it shut.

"Stop slamming the door, Destiny!" I heard dad's voice shout from the garage. The anger that used to bubble up inside of me no longer existed. I was already used to having him yell at me, and even if I hadn't been, the shock of the fall had left me paralyzed.

Before I could climb upstairs, my angry dad emerged from the garage. "Why are you late?" he demanded.

"I missed the bus," I lied. "I had to walk."

His face hardened in question. "Why didn't you drive to school this morning?"

"I don't have any more money for gas."

My dad's raging features transformed into a laughing tease. "So all of your friends made it to the bus except you? You're so brain-dead."

I fought back without noticing. "My teacher kept me inside the classroom to finish up classwork. How does that give you the right to call me brain-dead?"

His amused expression darkened. "I'm your father. I can call you whatever I want."

I ignored anything else he had to say and ascended the stairs. I vaguely heard his foul words echoing behind me.

I slammed my bedroom door shut, locked it, and ignored his demands to stop slamming the damn doors.

I let my balance falter, and I landed on the bed. Burying my face in my white pillow, I let the tears fall. I had almost died.

Died.

How could I have been so exposed? How could I not have noticed how effortlessly—how straightforwardly—life could be taken? I'd fallen into vulnerability without so much as noticing.

I lifted my head from my pillow, examining the wet fabric. I wiped my nose with the back of my sleeve. Every time I tried pulling myself together, I just fell apart again. The anguish built itself up inside my chest, making me clench my teeth, unable to hold back.

In my mind, I created my own world—a world where

everything was right. I had my mom back, my dad and Jade were gone, and Jared ... Jared ...

The dream shattered.

What had happened to Jared?

I knew he could escape the government fighter jets, but what about the silhouette? What *was* the silhouette? The questions distracted my tears, thankfully.

The questions swirled around my head so fast that I thought I heard buzzing in my ears. I realized it was my phone vibrating. Still shaking from my crying and feeling that my mouth was dry like cotton, I thought about hitting END, but then I read the caller's name and immediately hit ANSWER.

"Crystal?" I shouted as if I'd seen Mom's ghost.

"Destiny, where did you go? You abandoned me! I was waiting for you at the car. Did you walk home? You know, you could've told me." Crystal's demanding Brooklyn accent screamed through the earpiece. I pulled the phone away from my head to save my ear from the abuse.

"Sorry, Crystal." I sighed, putting the phone back to my ear. "I got a bit distracted."

"Distra—?" It didn't take her long to find out what I meant. "What's this? You never told me you were going out with someone! Who's the guy?"

As Crystal was talking, I wasn't really paying much attention. My main thoughts were on my near death. I wanted so badly to tell someone about what happened, but I knew better than to open my mouth and risk unwanted government ears hearing.

"Did my loud squawking make you deaf or something?" Crystal's voice brought me back to the present.

"Sorry, Crystal. I just—"

"Ah, I see. You know, I think you're friend-sick. Tell you what, I'll come and pick you up in ten. What do you say to a movie?"

"Which one?"

"Whichever—your choice."

I wiped away the remaining tears dribbling down my face. A movie would probably take my mind off of what happened earlier, but Jared had warned me to not leave the house. But with my dad probably having an itchy leather belt hand, I *needed* to get out. Besides, it was only the movies. I would only be gone for a few hours or so.

I would have to sneak past my dad.

"Don't park in front of my house. My dad will see you. Meet me a few blocks out of sight."

"Meet you there. Bye, girlie."

Crystal hung up before I did, and I reluctantly slipped out of bed and pulled on a white T-shirt and faded jeans. After throwing on a black Breaking Benjamin sweater, I quickly ran my fingers through my hair in lieu of brushing, sprayed perfume in the air, and walked through it for a light berry scent. I glanced in the mirror and forced a fake smile onto my face.

I swiped up my purse as I headed out bedroom door. I had just made it downstairs and twisted the doorknob when Dad's serene voice sounded behind me. "Where do you think you're going?"

"Out," I replied, cloaking the explosive malice in my voice with a cool tone.

"Where's 'out'?" He sounded almost challenging, as if he thought he could keep me locked up in here forever.

I turned to face him. "I'm going for a walk."

My dad's eyes darkened. "Don't think you're going anywhere after what you just did to me." My dad jabbed his finger toward the stairs. "Go back to your room and don't come out until it's time for you to make me dinner."

"*What I just did to you?* I came home late because I missed the bus."

"Back-talking now?" His hands reached for his belt.

Reacting on instinct, I whirled around and ran away upstairs, locked my door, and reached for my phone to cancel the movie with Crystal.

But then I stopped myself, my eyes settling on the window. A thick branch that spouted from a large sycamore grazed the sill of the window.

MIST CLUNG TO THE AIR and the cold pricked my skin like needles as I walked along the side of the road leading to the entrance of the community. As I peered ahead, I noticed the sky had taken on a slight orange haze, the sun nestled halfway under the hills and grassland.

I breathed in the clean air that mingled with the scent of

freshly cut lawns, glad to be out of the house. It was always so dank and clammy in there, even though it was a two-story. The rooms are dust infested, and my dad always leaves his room a mess, as if he expects me to clean it when I get back from school. Life wouldn't suck this badly if Mom was still here.

I shook the thought from my head. Mom was dead, and I would just have to deal with it. Nothing could bring her back. I'd just have to soldier on whether I liked it or not.

Three years may have passed since she died, but not a day slipped past that I haven't felt a small feeling of dread in some hollow corner of myself. I guessed it was normal, especially since I had an abusive dad.

I rounded a curve, jogged up a block, and spotted Crystal's car parked near the edge of the sidewalk with the windows rolled down.

Like always, she had her rock music turned up to full blast. I hurriedly opened the car door and slumped in the passenger seat.

"Hey, girlie," Crystal sang as she turned down the radio volume. Sunglasses shaded her eyes, but I could feel her enthusiasm as if it were bursting and oozing from the music.

"Hi, Crystal." My voice cracked a little, but I regained my composure.

Crystal pulled down her glasses. "Destiny." She sounded like she just saw me give away a hundred dollars.

"You look cool with that outfit." I admired her black lace-up corset top with navy high-waisted skinny jeans. "Did you get it from Hot Topic?" I tried to lead a conversation elsewhere.

Crystal didn't stop staring at me. "You don't look so hot. Are you okay?"

I rested the back of my head against the seat. "Let's go and try to catch a movie. I'm fine." What an effortless white lie it was.

Crystal began to drive slowly, gradually picking up the pace, but she looked like she didn't want to ignore me. She caught the idea that I was trying to avoid talking about what happened and that it would be better off staying that way.

We exited the neighborhood and joined traffic on the open streets.

Crystal picked at another subject. "Sooo, let's hear about your boyfriend!"

My stomach twisted at the thought of my near-death experience with Jared. I looked out the window in a motion that said I didn't want to talk about that either.

"What?" She sucked her teeth. "Don't tell me you broke up the first day meeting."

I instantly jumped into conversation at this remark. "We didn't break up, we just ... we're still together, but it's just that this ... *thing* ... happened, and now I'm a little shaky. That's all."

Crystal sighed, visibly exasperated with my lack of detail. She shut off the low-volume radio. "Destiny, if it's bothering you so much, just tell me what it is."

How would I just dump all this on her?

Our conversation crashed when the Regal Cinema came into sight. The parking lot was full, and nearly all the spaces were taken. Crystal veered the car into a tight parking space, and we swung out in a hurry to get to the concession stand for tickets before the lines grew too long.

By the time we made it to the front, Crystal brought up a subject I had completely forgotten about. "What movie should we see? I don't know about you, but I'm in the mood for something action-packed, with *lots* of near deaths and drama."

I think I'm going to puke.

"Uh ..." I gave the now-playing movie list a long, ambiguous gaze. "Let's see something more slow-paced, like ... romance." My gaze fell upon *Safe Haven.* I'd seen the trailer several times and had wanted to watch it for a while.

Crystal stared at me. "That's the worst way to take your mind off something. What you need is *action.*" She grabbed me by the shoulders, shaking me slightly. "We're at the movies, girl! Get excited!"

I smiled embarrassedly, even though my heart was pounding briskly against my chest. I brushed her hands off me. "Stop it. Fine, we'll see action."

Crystal slammed her palms on the counter in a thrilled position and spoke into the microphone. "Two tickets for *Parker*!"

The woman behind the glass stared at us as if we'd just called her grandma. "Sure. That'll be twenty sixty-six."

I handed Crystal eleven dollars, and she slid the rest of the money into the tray, swiping the tickets.

After ordering extra-buttery popcorn and soda, we found the screen room at the end of the hallway, and the lights began to dim as we walked in. The popcorn filled my nose with a buttery, creamy scent, but I wasn't hungry at all, even though I had skipped lunch.

Crystal seemed to know *every* technique when it came to movies. Never get a seat in the front, because you'd have to crank your head up painfully to see the screen. Sit in the back, and you'd be too far away from the movie, and people's heads would be blocking most of it from your view. Don't come in too early, or else you'd have to sit there and wait for the advertisements to finish, and by the time the movie starts, you're all out of popcorn and soda.

Crystal and I squeezed ourselves through a row of seats, grabbed two chairs in the center, and watched the crowd of people strolling in, catching the best seats they could. In the dark, I saw Crystal's smile widen. "Just in time."

Chapter 4

CAPTURED

An uneasy feeling crawled up inside me as the lights grew dimmer and the movie began to play. I leaned forward and clutched my stomach in apprehension.

"Destiny?" I knew Crystal was sitting right next to me, but she sounded miles away. "I knew it. Something is *definitely* wrong."

I swallowed, but it didn't reduce the swimming stomach acid. "I'm fine." My voice cracked.

"Girlie, go to the bathroom just in case." Crystal reached for my shoulder but recoiled, as if afraid I'd puke all over her. "I'll wait for you."

I somberly nodded my head, and grabbing the seats for balance, I stumbled out of the theater and scanned the dimly lit corridors for a restroom sign. I spotted one of the employees sweeping up popcorn from the red carpet floor.

"Excuse me, could you tell me where the restroom is?" I asked, strolling up to him while trying to hide my vertigo.

"Sure, just head that way." He pointed down the hall I had just come down. "There'll be a door that leads outside. The restroom should be in the next building."

"Thanks," I mumbled, unable to speak louder, afraid that the bile would find its way up.

Following the man's directions, I shoved the door open, peered around the alley, and saw the restroom sign. The cold wind stung my skin, worsening my sickening feeling and producing a thick layer of goose bumps on my skin. I snuggled deeper into my thin, black sweater that did nothing much against the sheer cold.

I sauntered toward the bathroom, the empty street making the night seem even more dangerous than it already was—which wasn't a good thing, considering there were no security cameras out here. Oily puddles of water dampened the cement, and old, chewed-up black gum dotted the pavement. Graffiti was sprayed across the brick walls in a jumble of fat letters and cartoons.

A horrible stench filled my nose, making my stomach churn more than it already had been. I just had to wash my face—maybe it would lessen the shock. I doubted it.

I can't believe I'm doing this. I need help. I need someone to talk to. I need to see Jared. I need—

My thoughts were interrupted when someone grabbed my shoulder from behind.

My blood froze, and I whirled around, fear allowing me to expect the worst. Instead, I came face-to-face with some guy in a T-shirt and jeans.

"Relax," he said. "I just want to ask you something."

Ask me something? Is he insane?

His voice was reassuring, and a small hint of gentleness was detectable in it. Even so, something about him wasn't quite right, something I couldn't put my finger on. I could almost feel the air around him crackle with a dangerous charge.

I stepped back, keeping my distance. "Who are you?" I cloaked all fear in my voice with resolve.

The man reached into his pocket, fished out a wallet, flicked it open, and revealed a ... business card?

No. An ID.

"My name is Carlos Law, undercover elite investigator of the Government's Suspect Investigating Task Force." He flipped the wallet shut. "I believe you know something you shouldn't."

Anxiety burned in my chest at these words.

How had they found me? They hadn't seen my license plate, they couldn't have tracked me with my phone, since I didn't have it with me at the beach, and I hadn't even taken my car out of the garage! What had given me away?

Carlos seemed to read my thoughts. "We've done our research, and observation tells us—"

I cut him off. "*Observation?* You've been *following* me?"

Carlos ignored my abrupt question and continued on.

"Observation tells us that one person has been visiting *Windpoint Beach* extremely frequently, even before the incident," he said, enunciating "Windpoint Beach" as if it rang a bell, but I hid my awareness. "That person's name is Destiny Aubrey. We researched the name and found one person who lives nearest to Windpoint, and that led us to you." He grabbed my arm. "You're coming with me."

I flinched at his sudden movement and yanked my arm back. "Don't touch me," I hissed. I wasn't entirely surprised at my cynical aggressiveness. After everything that had happened over the past two days, anyone would have expected me to keep my guard up, no matter what the situation.

Carlos's eyes narrowed, and he seized my wrists. "Don't make this hard on yourself, Destiny." His calm voice had darkened.

I struggled in his iron grip, trying desperately to wrench free, but no avail.

Jared! I screamed through my thought channels, hoping Jared could hear me, wherever he was. *Jared! Help me!*

I managed to wrestle my right hand from his grasp, but he caught it again. He pulled my arms painfully behind my back, and I heard the *clink* of steel handcuffs binding my wrists. I thrashed around in his clutches, but his strength was far stronger than mine.

Compelled by defensiveness, I drove my foot straight between his legs, causing him to double over.

Taking advantage of his immobility, I tried running out of the alley, but my hands were still cuffed behind me.

I lost my balance and fell.

Before I could get up and continue running, Carlos kneeled over me, throwing me into a standing position and holding me in place. I tried to scream, but Carlos's hand was cupped over my mouth, silencing me.

In my line of vision, I saw a black Honda Civic slow to a stop on the curb at the end of the alleyway. A cloth bag was pulled down over my head, and I felt Carlos lead me to the vehicle. I heard a trunk open, and I was thrown inside. Pure darkness ate into my vision.

Jared! I screeched in my mind. *They found us! They know who I am! They kidnapped me!* I swallowed. The word *kidnapped* made me cringe in fear.

I kept shouting through my mind, trying to reach Jared, but either he couldn't hear me, or ...

A sudden thought of the killer shadow I'd seen earlier ran through my mind. It was then that I realized that Jared might not have gotten away from it. What if the creature caught him? What if—?

I felt the driver suddenly step on it, and the Honda lurched into drive.

Instinctively, I brought my feet up and kicked against the trunk door, in a sad attempt to break it open. I screamed, protested, and threw out all the profanity I knew, but Carlos and the driver ignored me completely.

My heart raced uncontrollably. What were they going to do? Where was the driver going?

Interrogation?

Captivity?

Prison?

For once, I didn't even want to know.

The car vibrated as it moved, and if I listened closely enough, I could hear the faint sound of tires rolling over gravel, indicating that we were far from city life.

I vaguely heard Carlos and the driver deep in conversation. I couldn't make out most of their words, but I gathered just enough information to get an idea of what they were talking about.

"Girl—destiny—dark angel—need— where—she knows." In my head I provided the missing pieces myself.

They knew I knew about Jared, the dark angel. They needed information from me to know where he was. I was the only one who knew.

I bit my bottom lip to hold back the tears. I had never wanted this. I fell in love with Jared, but at the cost of being abducted by the government. They were going to ask me questions I couldn't answer. I didn't know where Jared was.

Suddenly, the Honda came to a stop, slamming my body against the back of the trunk.

I heard the driver shriek in terror. "What the hell?" he shouted.

The next thing I knew, something large and powerful slammed into the hood of the car, making it bounce and rock. I heard the driver and passenger doors fly open, and the sound of gunshots made me jolt.

I heard the sharp *snap* that could only have been a neck and then a cry of horror.

"Stay away from me!" I heard Carlos scream before he flung himself into the car, and I heard a glove compartment open, followed by the rushing sound of him trying to reload his weapon.

Several crushing smashes sounded, and Carlos's pleas grew silent.

Confused and terrified, I shook the cloth bag from my head and listened for anything else.

Suddenly, something slammed against the trunk door, slightly cracking it. A small streak of moonlight poured through the gap, and I saw a very familiar silhouette on the other side.

Jared threw the trunk door off its hinges and pulled me into a tight embrace. He pulled away and grasped my shoulders, firing questions at me. "Are you hurt? Did they touch you? What did they do?"

At that moment, tears welled up behind my eyes, and I was unable to hold them back. "Jared, I'm—they—I'm fine, but—"

Jared took hold of the handcuffs that dug into my skin and snapped them both in half, releasing my wrists. I rubbed my hands, which now had red marks from the cold steel.

Tears blurred my lower line of vision as I clung onto him, sobbing into his chest. I didn't know how much more of this I could take.

Jared murmured reassuring whispers into my ear. "Cupid, it's okay. I'm here. I'm here. You're okay." He pressed a kiss to my forehead.

Jared tilted my head up, his eyes silently watching mine, but I pulled away, too shocked to do anything.

"I told you to stay at home. It's not safe to go out. Why did you ignore my warning?" Jared's voice didn't seem angry or even remotely disappointed. Instead, he sounded worried, distressed.

"Jared, I'm sorry. I—it's just—I mean—" My body was shaking so much, and my speech was reduced to racketing words between portions of broken sentences.

Jared silenced me with a smooth shush of his lips. "It's okay. We'd better get out of here. This is the last place we want to be seen together."

I gave an unsteady nod as a reply, and Jared scooped me in up into his arms. His black wings ruptured from his back, and we were flying from the scene as fast as possible.

Question time.

"What was that?" I asked, looking up at him in hopes of being led to an answer.

I held Jared's gaze, which was swallowed up by all-consuming dread. "Two government agents kidnapped you in hopes of forcing you to give them information about me."

I shook my head. "Not what I meant."

Jared's features hardened, and I knew he was remembering that black shadow. I noticed he was deep in thought, and it didn't look like he would come out. "Jared? What is it?"

Jared's hold on me instinctively tightened. "They want to take me away from you. I've spent more time here than I should have."

I hated being left in suspense. "Jared, what the hell is it?"

Jared held me tighter, as if afraid that I would vanish from his embrace. "I've seen this happen with other dark angels. They have this ... *thing* follow them, stalk them, chase them, until they're caught."

Jared didn't need to finish his sentence to fill in the gap. Somehow, I managed to know what he was going to say. He looked down at me as I snuggled deeper into his warm, protective arms.

"It doesn't want to harm you. It wants me to leave the Mortal Realm. It thinks I'm going to hurt you."

"Does *it* have a name?"

Jared moaned. "We call them battle-bloods. And there are many more of different species out there."

"So if they chase dark angels, then that means they're on the light side?"

"No. They're the exact opposite of that. They try to collect as many dark angels as they can to add to their—" He paused. I gave him an expectant look to continue, but instead, he said, "I'm giving you too much information. For our sake, I can't tell you everything. If the government is trying to arrest you, you can't know much about us."

I looked down at the trees and grassland that were now materializing into city life. Jared was about to mention something crucial, but I couldn't know too much because the government could squeeze out information never supposed to be known. "So, they're called battle-bloods, right? And they want to collect as many dark angels as they can?"

Jared sighed, looking back to make sure we weren't being followed. "Yes. They're battle-bloods. And the one chasing me is dangerous. I almost didn't get away from it."

My heart was still racing and I tried unsuccessfully to slow it. "The government knows who I am, where I live, and where I've been. On top of that, we have a demon shadow that's out for your blood. What do we do now?"

Jared's eyes roamed me with silent heat. "Now, we run as far as we can go."

Chapter 5

RESPITE

Run as far as we can go? Was he serious? After a few days of knowing Jared, I could see that almost nothing he said was serious. But if we were to go on pursuit, we would need to be prepared. We couldn't just decide to go on the run. Jared's wings picked up speed in a worried gesture, even though we weren't being followed.

I felt like pushing away from him in disbelief, but we were hundreds of feet in the air. I fixed him with a shocked expression. *What do you mean by "run"? Is this your idea of a crude joke?* I wasn't hesitant with my outward ruthlessness. If he thought I was just going to drop everything and just run away, he was wrong. *How can we just leave? We're not even ready!*

Jared looked down at me with a concerned but understanding gaze. *I know you're not prepared and you can't just come along with me. I never planned for this, much less thought this through if the problem actually sprung up. If there's one thing I know about those people, it's that they're persistent. They won't stop until they've got the job done.*

I fixed my attention to the buildings below. Pedestrians were walking the streets, unaware of Jared flying with me in the skies. *So that's it, then. We have no choice. We have to run. Lucky for you, you don't have to pack or leave anything behind. Me, I've got all my clothes at home, my iPhone, and—* I realized something that made me sigh in irritation. *Crystal's still waiting for me at the movie theater.*

We have to forget about Crystal, Jared replied. *Sorry, but we're in a life-or-death situation right now.*

I know that, but I'm just saying—my dad will notice that I've been gone for too long. He'll try to call me, but I won't answer because I left my purse with Crystal. He'll call the cops, they'll realize I'm the daughter who saved the dark angel and question my dad, and he'll tell them he doesn't know where I— I stopped my thought, realizing the most horrible thing.

What is it? Jared asked quickly.

My dad has my phone tracker. He'll track down my phone to Crystal. Oh my god, I hope she leaves the theater and forgets my purse.

If she doesn't, they still won't know where we are. If we get going in the next hour, we can get a head start, and since it's nighttime, they'll have a harder time spotting us, Jared said, spreading his wings to descend.

Where are we going? I asked.

It's getting late, and I've hadn't had rest in weeks. If we were to start running now, my exhaustion might slow us down, and that's something I don't want to risk, Jared replied with the slightest tone of tiredness. It was then that I actually decided to take a good look at his face.

Lines of weariness engraved his features, red tinged the bottom of his eyes, and his black hair was a mass of tangles. I'd only gotten ten-minute chances to be with him, and because of those slim meetings, it had never actually come to my mind that he hadn't had a decent sleep in such a long time. How could I not have noticed?

To shake the awful feeling off my thoughts, I revised my question. *So where are you planning to stay? We can't go back home. Won't we have them looking for us?*

I know that, and that's why we're not heading back home. We've got to spend the night somewhere where they won't be expecting. Jared spread his wings out to descend, and his feet landed behind some kind of hotel I didn't recognize.

"What are we doing here? This is the first place the government will look." I knew Jared liked to play around and was a master at sarcasm, but was he really going to stay at a hotel—the only building that stood out among the rest of places we could stay?

"That's why I'm going to deceive the desk clerk into thinking we're some other people. If any investigators come, he'll say he hasn't seen anyone register all day."

I loved it when he did that.

Jared tucked his wings in, and they vanished. I started strolling to the front door, but Jared stopped me in midstride and pressed us up against the wall, keeping us hidden from people on the street. I had to get used to this. No more walking out in the center of attention.

Jared peered around the corner, keeping an eye out for any suspicious people. When he seemed to find none, he clasped my hand and led me inside through the front doors.

Hotel Indigo read the lit-up blue sign above the doors. As we stepped in, everything was just as I wasn't expecting.

Three couch-chairs circled a table with a pile of magazines that sat lazily on the dust-free marble. The walls were tattooed with something that looked somewhat fancy, large black chandeliers hung from the circular ceiling, and a wooden registration desk that was painted to look gold stood on the other end of the room, a desk clerk sitting behind it. The flooring was patterned with tile marble that sparkled in the light of the chandeliers and lamps that illuminated a silvery tint.

"Can I help you?" The desk clerk's voice carried me back to reality. She looked to be eighteen, and she wore a tight uniform made out of burlap that looked uncomfortable, even if worn for a few seconds. A Mac computer sat on the edge of the desk.

"Yeah, we'd like to register a one-room. Highest floor you have available," Jared ordered in a tone that told the desk clerk we were in a hurry. I knew he'd chosen the highest floor so that if government agents tried to chase us upstairs, we could easily fly off the roof and escape ... if they didn't bring helicopters.

The desk clerk got to the point and powered on the laptop. After a few clicks on the keyboard, she announced, "All right, looks like you have a room available on the top floor. Your room number will be 1047." She plucked a set of keys attached to a plastic tab with the room number off the wall behind her and handed them to Jared. "Here are your keys."

Jared tucked the keys into his leather jacket, and the desk clerk took one long stare at him from head to toe. I felt a sudden stab of possessiveness.

"Can I help you find your room?" she said in an almost flirty tone.

"No thanks," Jared said, wrapping his arm around me. "I think we can manage to find it ourselves."

The clerk's eyes darted from me to Jared. "Oh, so you two are together? I didn't know." Her voice trailed off when she saw my darkened expression. She had done that right in front of me!

The thunder booming outside matched my outrage. I could faintly hear the rain falling down in heavy sheets outside.

Jared leaned in and took one long stare into the clerk's eyes, and she immediately froze. I could hear her heart pounding as if someone were playing drums in the room. "If any government investigators ask, we're not here." His eyes were darkened with the murkiest gray I've ever seen, almost black. It took me a moment to realize he was deceiving her.

Jared quickly added, "And give us a free room."

I rolled my eyes at his ability to maintain a playful attitude in a serious situation.

Jared pulled away, and his eyes reverted to normal. The desk clerk blinked and relaxed her stance, as if nothing had happened. "Enjoy your stay."

Jared led me up the stairs and down the hall. Finding our designated room, he double locked the door behind us. I took a good look around the room. A long desk with a LED screen TV stood on one side of the room, facing one king-size bed. Chips, nuts, and whiskey and other beverages sat in a neat order on the desk. Two bedside tables encased both sides of the bed, and a sliding glass door led to a balcony that overlooked the parking lot. I drew back the curtains draping over the window and frowned at the storm blowing outside in the night.

I stepped into the bathroom, and to my surprise, the floor was heated. The walls were white, patterned with blue diamond tiles. The shower had a transparent curtain drawn around it, blurring anything behind it, and the sink had a pink ring around the bowl.

Behind me, Jared pulled me closer to him. "Now we have some time alone."

My eyes wandered to the floor. "I still don't think this is such a good idea."

"Stop worrying. I already deceived the desk clerk into not blowing our cover."

"But what if they have security cameras outside? What if someone saw us go in? What if—?"

Jared cut me off with a finger to my lips. "Cupid, there's nothing to worry about. Nobody was outside, there were no security cameras, and my deceiving has never failed before. End of story."

Jared sat me down at the foot of the bed. "Nothing's going to hurt you as long as I'm here."

Once he assumed he'd gotten enough assurance into me, he stood up and scratched the back of his head. "I need a shower. I haven't had a decent one in weeks." A flirty smile crept up to his mouth. "Then I'll meet you in bed."

My heart jumped in my throat.

"Relax, it's not like I'm going to complicate things in this situation." Jared had read my mind again ... or at least my face.

Jared stepped inside the bathroom, leaving the door slightly ajar. I heard him pull back the curtain and turn the shower on. Steam flowed through the gap in the bathroom door, and for the sake of civility, I shut it.

I collapsed on the bed, snatched up the remote, and flipped through channels. My old TV in my room didn't even have half these stations. Finding no program I even knew of, I switched it to the news and pressed my head against back the pillow, trying to shake the feeling that something wasn't right—indeed, that something was going to go terribly wrong.

Jared emerged from the bathroom, steam flowing around his ankles. He was shirtless, wearing only a pair of jeans and a towel draped across his left shoulder. The news anchor's words suddenly seemed distant.

"Bet you can't resist this." Jared pressed his arms against

the back of his neck, closed his eyes, and tilted his head backwards. He opened one eye at me to make sure I was looking. I couldn't help myself. I burst into a fit of laughter.

WE'D GONE TO SLEEP HOURS ago, and the storm had not let up. Jared woke up several times in the night, saying he'd heard something. Each time it took several minutes for him to fall asleep again. But falling asleep wasn't as easy as it sounded in a storm like this.

Jared had his arm tucked beneath me, almost protectively. He had just said his deceiving never failed. What could be making him so nervous?

More than once, I heard a strange rattling noise by the window, but I passed it off as the wind blowing some tree branches against it. I rolled to my right, and my blood froze when I saw someone's silhouette staring at us through the window. Lightning illuminated the room, and the figure vanished.

No way in hell could that have been the battle-blood chasing Jared. Hadn't he lost it after our private flight? I blinked several times, but the figure didn't reappear. I shook the horrible thoughts from my head as a product of my imagination and closed my eyes, trying unsuccessfully to beckon sleep. I flopped to my left, staring into a mirror plastered on a wall. This time, I screamed.

The battle-blood was back outside the window, clawing at the glass like a spider.

My scream woke Jared with a start, his eyes frantically darting around the room. "Destiny, what is it?"

I whirled back to the window, and the battle-blood had disappeared once again. Jared followed my gaze, and wearily stepped out of bed before walking barefoot to the window to see what was out there.

"Jared, be careful," I whispered, still trembling from shock.

Jared drew back the curtains a bit, keeping himself hidden. If there was one thing he knew about that creature, was that it liked to play games. Deadly games.

I suddenly remembered my childhood fear of the darkness. My mom would drag a chair in front of the closet door, lock up the windows, and keep the bedroom door slightly open, allowing the light to pour in. She never really bought me a nightlight. If she had, I'd have gotten used to it and would never have grown out of it.

In this situation, I really wish mastering fears was that easy—especially since this fear was a nightmare brought to reality.

I sluggishly stepped off the bed, the tile flooring ice-cold against my feet. I moved closer to the window and saw something dart across the lawn below. Then the battle-blood smashed itself into the window. I almost fell backwards in surprise. Jared threw the curtains back and grabbed my wrist, pulling me to the door. "We need to get out of here. *Now.*"

Jared's fingers barely touched the doorknob before something else slammed into the door from the hall outside. I ambled backward. There were two battle-bloods.

We were trapped.

The battle-bloods repeatedly slammed into the windows and doors. They were trying to get in, but why couldn't they? Jared answered my silent question.

"The reason I chose this specific room was because it has the most technology from the outside. If they try to attack us, they can't get in." He developed black wings from his back in a gesture of preparedness for battle. He folded his arms around me and led me back to the bed.

"What if they bring reinforcements?" I had no idea how stupid that sounded. "What if it's not just the two of them?"

"They won't," Jared replied, the crashes getting stronger, louder. "The largest number they travel in is groups of two."

I pulled myself closer to him in fear of what might happen, listening to one crash after another. "What if you're wrong? What if—?"

Jared cut me off with a soft kiss on my lips. His mouth lightly brushed mine and then pressed against it, warm and bold. My heart ignited from a tiny ember into a wild flame, despite my racing pulse. The loud crash of thunder reverberated in the night sky, threatening to tear the black heavens apart.

Jared's lips parted from mine. He gazed at me with sincere yet troubled eyes. "If anything happens tonight, I want to let you know that I love you."

I uttered a sob. "No. Don't say that. We'll survive this night. We'll be together. Please don't say that."

Jared cradled my head in his hands, keeping me secured against him.

Lightning flickered through the pitch-black room, lighting up his features, forming shadows that outlined his muscular shoulders. I enfolded my arms around his neck, pressing myself against him, my grip becoming stronger with each crash the battle-bloods produced.

I felt myself being pulled to him by some sort of invisible magnet that I had no power over, and it only toughened our emotional bond.

I wanted every last bit of him, even if that meant casting a deathly shadow over my life. As long as we were together, nothing else mattered. But then what would the future bring us?

Chapter 6

WINGBEATS

As I slowly floated back up to consciousness, I distinctly felt Jared's warm body heat close to mine. His arms were wrapped protectively around me, and the unbroken rise and fall of his chest made me smile. I closed my eyes and snuggled closer.

Light filtered through the window, illuminating a wall of floating dust in midair. I could distinctly hear the faint chirping of birds outside.

The battle-bloods had to leave sooner or later. I guess they were finally starting to accept that they couldn't get inside. The immense amount of wires on the outer wall of the hotel kept them out, but we still left the TV on and set the AC to full blast to increase the technology supply in the air around us.

Against all odds, the door resounded with a loud knocking. The sheets ruffled under Jared's movement as he rested his head on my shoulder. He grumbled as he fell back into the clutches of sleep. Neither of us tried to get up to answer the door. It was probably just the maid.

The knocking grew louder, more constant, until I couldn't just ignore it. "Jared," I murmured. "Jared, the maid's knocking."

Jared replied with a groan.

"Jared, answer the door."

He didn't respond.

I sighed, threw the sheets off me, and reluctantly got out of bed, rubbing my eyes wearily. I took one last look at Jared, his arms still splayed across the sunken hole in the mattress where my body had been. I assumed Jared hadn't gotten much sleep last night, and he would need as much as he could get. I had fallen asleep before he did, and it must've taken him time to find rest. Who knew how long?

I stumbled to the door and opened it. "Sorry, we're not ready to—" I shrieked and shut the door in their faces.

My sudden cry woke Jared up with a start. "What happened? They came back?"

I pointed to the door. "No, but—who the hell are those people outside?"

I didn't want to sound like the crazy old lady with a hundred cats, but I kept receiving these surges of defiance and self-defense. After Carlos Law had kidnapped me, I didn't know who or what to expect. If I let my guard down, I let my life down.

Jared stared at me. "People?" He tugged on a shirt and jeans and swung open the door. "Hey, Nick. 'Sup, Demonica."

I made my way to the door and peered through. The boy, obviously named Nick, had short brown hair, deep-set eyes, low eyebrows, a narrow nose, and a husky build. He looked to be slightly older than I was. He wore a bloodred T-shirt and black jeans, his hands clasped inside the deep pockets.

My attention shifted to Demonica, who was no younger than Nick. She had blonde hair, sea green eyes, a black shirt and black pants, and these insane curves that made me tremble with jealousy. Her features resembled those of a cat's: minor and delicate with high cheekbones—nothing short of a professional skank. She obviously had all the time in the world for the gym.

But what were they doing here?

"Jared, why are they here? Nobody is supposed to know where we are. If we get caught—"

"I called them over." Jared replied in a tone that sounded like he was trying to reassure me.

"Why?"

"They've had to deal with situations like this before. They can help us." Jared spoke with such seriousness that I thought I'd heard him say something else. They'd dealt with this? Help us? Wait, then that would mean ...

"You guys are dark angels?" I tilted my head and blinked a few times, trying to see their wings.

Demonica shook her head. "Do we look like dark angels?"

Ah. So she was a true jerk. Her sassy, conceited voice only supported that theory.

"We're fallen." Nick spoke over her, as if trying to excuse her impoliteness. I didn't think it was working. Nick grimaced, and eyes swept down the halls, as if looking for something. "We should talk more about this inside."

Jared understood what he was saying. He swung the door open wider and let them in, giving the hallways one last cautious look before closing the door.

I sat down at the foot of the bed, next to Jared. Nick leaned against the doorframe, one arm wrapped around Demonica's waist. She shot me a cynical smile. To block my anger, I changed the subject. "Wait. So why did you guys fall?"

Nick grunted. "We got sick and tired of having that thing chasing us."

I stared at him. That wasn't been the answer I had been expecting.

"If a dark angel falls, then the creature loses interest in chasing him," Nick said, making it a bit clearer.

Letting this sink in, I looked up at Jared. We'd found a solution.

"But it comes with a cost," Nick announced quickly. "If Jared falls, he won't be able to feel anything. No sensation will be possible anymore."

I clenched my teeth. What was a better choice—stopping the creature or keeping Jared's sensation? I weighed the options in my hands, each leading to a completely different path, a completely different outcome, but both had the exact same weight. We couldn't be defeated this easily.

"What other choices do we have?" Jared asked.

Nick thought for a moment. "Well ... you can become human."

"What's the risk?" I sighed, not getting my hopes up.

Nick looked like he was having trouble giving it to me straight. I braced myself.

"If Jared wants to be mortal, he has to ... die"—he said the word as quickly as possible—"and be reborn a human."

A thick, heavy silence settled over the room, and my grip on Jared's hand instinctively tightened. I had heard him correctly, hadn't I? My thoughts were so loud that I could've sworn they were physically in the room, despite the silence.

Does Jared really have to die? Isn't there another way? There has to be.

Jared broke the silence. "How does a dark angel die? Aren't we immortal?"

"That's what the problem is. A dark angel can't die from a headshot or any other physical means. What they need is a sword that was made of celestial material." Nick went along uncomfortably, unlike Demonica. She just stared at me with eyes of selfishness and victory, as if she was enjoying watching me cringe.

"I thought celestial doesn't exist anywhere on earth," I said, recalling last week's history lesson. Wasn't that from Roman times?

Demonica sneered at me. "Dark angel feathers are made

of celestial. I never realized how illiterate female humans can get."

I so wanted to punch her.

I brushed a strand of hair away from my face. "So all we need is one of Jared's feathers to create a celestial sword?"

Nick shook his head, indicating that it got more complicated. I groaned.

"We need feathers from another dark angel," Nick said.

I molded together everything we had discussed. "So, in order for that thing to stop stalking us, Jared needs to be human. In order for Jared to be human, we need feathers from another dark angel."

A small grimace tugged at Nick's mouth. "Exactly."

I raised my hands and let them fall to my lap. "Well, this is going to be easy."

Jared nodded his head in agreement. "Finding another dark angel? Doesn't get any simpler."

Demonica sneered at me. "Finding a dark angel who's willing to give up one of their feathers is anything but easy. They'll put up a fight like no other human can. This has 'failure' written all over it."

Cold, fiery rage rippled through me. "We were being sarcastic."

Demonica scoffed and looked away with a conceited expression. "Well, I knew that. I was being sarcastic as well."

What?

"Well, we better get going," Jared announced as he got to his feet. The mattress rose from his movement.

"Get going?" I asked softly, trying to avoid Demonica's ears. "Where do we start?"

Jared gazed at me with soft eyes. "The one place where all dark angels are attracted to." He set his gaze on Nick. "Nick, you still remember the highway route to Los Angeles, right?"

Chapter 7

ADDICTION

L os Angeles wasn't far from Napa. From where I live, I was
looking at a ten-hour drive or bus ride. But the distance
wasn't the only problem. With the government looking
for us, we had to take extreme precautions. We couldn't all walk
out of the bus at the same time. We had to split up into groups,
get off at different stops, and then all meet up somewhere.

Before we left, I checked the bathroom to see if they had
toothbrushes, and to my surprise, they did. I grabbed two
toothbrushes wrapped in plastic and a tube of toothpaste and
followed the team out the door and down the hallway.

Jared led the way out of the hotel, deceiving the clerk at the
front desk as we walked through the doors. Bright sunlight
streamed into my eyes. I squinted, purple afterimages dancing

across my vision. Judging by the sun's position in the sky, I could tell that we had woken up pretty late, and I wondered if it would affect our trip to LA.

Trees and brushwood grew on one side of the road, giving off a crisp smell of oak and pine. From here on, city life gradually began to fade, overgrown by the thick branches and tangled weeds of wildlife and forestry.

Giving the empty roads a long, worried stare, I frowned, knowing we had a long way to go and that there was no turning back if we got caught or lost.

Lined up next to the hotel were gift shops for the tourists. Advertisements were slapped on the windows, blocking out most of the interiors. The only thing inviting about this place was the breakfast restaurants. The faintest smell of eggs and bacon swirled from the restaurant doors each time they were opened, filling my nose with the most delicious scent.

My stomach started grumbling, and the pangs of hunger gnawed and tore viciously at it. I hadn't eaten since breakfast yesterday, but I had sort of gotten used to it. My dad never really liked to go grocery shopping, so I ate whatever they served us in school. Some days I would go to McDonald's with Crystal—

I flushed Crystal from my thoughts and instead focused on Jared.

Should we stop by to get something to eat before we go? I asked, biting my lip to battle the emptiness in my stomach.

Why? Are you hungry? We can grab a meal if you want. I

could tell he was growing attentive to my needs, even through his voice in his thought channels.

I responded quickly. *Won't we be taking the risk of being seen by security cameras in the restaurants? This isn't as easy as it used to be.*

I know. But we're moving farther from city life, making the chances of surveillance slimmer.

What about the employees? Won't any government officials question them about seeing us?

I'll take care of them. Deceiving, remember?

Jared turned to the rest of the team and said, "Let's grab something to eat before we get going."

Nick somberly agreed with a wilted nod of his head. "I haven't eaten in forever, so my stomach hates me right now." He turned to Demonica. "Hungry?"

"Sure, whatever."

I really had to start getting used to her abrupt attitude.

Jared led the group to a restaurant where they served breakfast all day.

My mouth watered.

I've always wanted to get a taste of IHOP but never got the chance to. When I wanted to eat breakfast at home, my dad would just tell me to open the fridge and eat what we had. Often, all he brought home was beer and whiskey.

We ascended a few wooden steps that connected with a porch with benches aligned on the exterior of the restaurant. A neon light sign reading Open hung next to the glass door, and the floorboards creaked underneath our feet.

Jared opened the door to let us in first, followed by the ringing of a bell hung above it. Demonica tried to push past me, but Nick held her back, telling her to search the area for surveillance.

Well, that made me feel a little better.

The exterior of the restaurant had an old-timey look to it. The ceiling was made of wood, and several black-and-white pictures of IHOP from the sixties were hung on the walls. There were customers, but not enough for someone to hear our conversations.

Faint music played in the background from a familiar radio station. The strong aroma of maple syrup swirled from the kitchen, and pangs of hunger gnawed at my stomach again. I could only imagine having a plate of food in front of me.

A waiter with long brown hair and thin looks met us at the front door. "How many?" she asked.

"Four," Nick replied, keeping things short. We hoped that no one here would recognize my face if it reached the news. But even most people who watched the news didn't really pay any attention to the wanted faces that came on. Most people just forgot them.

Even with these advantages, Jared still deceived whoever got near us. He would paint a picture in their heads, making it look like we were other people.

The waiter led us to a booth next to a window sprinkled with water from last night's heavy rain. She slid four menus across the table and smiled at each of us, making me wonder how she could just do that all day without complaining.

"Can I get you anything to drink?" she asked, holding a pen and notebook, ready to scribble down whatever we threw at her.

"Yeah, we'll get two Cokes," Demonica ordered before I could say anything.

Jared turned to me.

"I'll just have water." My throat was parched, as were my lips.

"Same here." Jared ordered, extending his arm around my neck.

The waiter jotted this down. "All right, I'll be back with your drinks and to take your entrée orders. Anything else?"

"That'll be it." Jared's full attention shifted to Nick. Clearly, he had something on his mind and couldn't afford to have anyone else listening.

As the waiter left, Jared asked, "Any idea on how you guys are going to follow us? Fallen don't have wings. You guys can't fly."

"Exactly," Nick replied, though not a single trace of worry was detectable in his voice. "That's why we got a car."

I fixed him with a long gaze. "You never told us you had a car."

He shrugged. "Never had the right time to bring it up."

"Of course we brought a car." Demonica sent me a low sneer. "How do you think we got here?"

I ignored her and gazed out over the parking lot through the window. "Where?"

Nick pointed to a blue Honda Civic parked at the edge of

the lot. "Since most cars are laced with technology, I picked out one that contained the least."

The windows were tinted, so no one would be able to see who was inside—perfect for running and hiding from the government.

My hunger suddenly reminded me why I was here. I opened the menu, frantically roaming through everything they had. The pictures of the food and the scent flowing out of the kitchen only worsened my hunger, making me wonder how long it would take for us to get the food.

"This looks good," I said, showing Jared the menu. "Whole wheat crepes with blueberries." I spoke in a low voice to avoid Demonica overhearing and cracking some crude joke. I wondered why Jared had even bothered to bring her along. She probably had more experience with governmental conflicts than Nick, allowing Jared to believe that she was useful for these types of tasks.

Jared took a swift look at the menu. "You want it, I'll get it. Anything for you." His eyes moved my way, a trademark flash of pleasure sparking in them.

I blushed, now knowing that nothing he said was a lie when it came to me.

Nick turned to Demonica. "You don't want anything?"

"I already ate." Demonica shook her head.

The waiter returned with four drinks balanced on a tray. "Here are your drinks. Are you guys ready to order?"

"Yeah, we'll have whole wheat crepes with blueberries and

double strawberry pancakes," Jared requested, not taking his eyes off mine.

"I'll have the Friday waffle combo." Nick ordered, his eyes still glued to the menu.

The waiter quickly noted the orders. "Be right back."

Please tell me you're being literal, I thought, clutching my stomach again.

We really needed to be careful around people. At least the TV was off so no one could see the news, and Jared was deceiving the waiter. But problems were still floating in the air around us. If we were going to drive all the way to Los Angeles, we needed to make sure no one else knew.

"So how are we getting there?" I asked.

Nick shifted his attention back to me. "We get in the car and we drive. I've gone there more times than I could count, so there's no need to worry."

Jared's eyes were cold and expression was determined. "Do we need to get the feathers from a specific dark angel, or can it be anyone?"

Nick leaned on the table to avoid anyone else listening in on the conversation. "It can't just be anyone. We need an angel who's become dark just recently. Someone in his thirties would also be perfect."

I wondered why dark angels were attracted to places like Los Angeles. Then I just remembered Demonica could also read my thoughts.

Demonica fixed me with an irritated glare, as if annoyed with my legion of questions. "Los Angeles has places like casinos and bars. Dark angels are drawn there like a moth to a light—thought you should know that."

"Since there are so many immortals in the area, the technology in the air wouldn't be so effective on them," Nick added in. "The large crowds can also help all of us remain unseen."

I nodded. "So then this could give us a good advantage."

"Almost. Los Angeles is a mix of dark angels, fallen, and humans. It's going to be hard to point out which is which. We'll need to isolate them to find out."

"As long as we get the job done." I felt Jared's hand clasp mine under the table.

We instantly shut down the conversation when the waiter reappeared with the food. We ate in silence, our thoughts focused on nothing but the mission—though half of mine were of nothing but Jared. My heart beat faster every time I glanced at him, but not from affection.

I knew this was going to be dangerous, but I couldn't see any other way. What if something got in our way? What if something happened to me and Jared?

I shook the horrible thought from my head, trying to focus on our advantages. Jared was immortal, so nothing could kill him. But if he turned human, he would be vulnerable. He could dye his hair and wear different clothes after he became human. We could slip past the government more easily, and the silhouette would no longer hunt him.

Breakfast went by slower than we had intended.

Jared stood up from the booth just as the waiter sauntered

to our table with the check. His eyes pierced into hers, and he murmured a command to let us walk out without paying.

I sighed. "Jared, could we please be civilized for once?"

"Hmm?" Jared murmured while simultaneously deceiving the waiter.

"Let's just pay for the food." I didn't want to grow a habit of taking food whenever I wanted. Jared wouldn't be able to do it anymore when he turned human, so we had to start breaking our habits now.

"She's right," I heard Nick agree behind me. "If we keep deceiving people, the government will start to see a trail where we've been. We'll be followed."

Jared thought for a moment before his eyes relaxed and his arms slackened. I could tell deceiving took a lot of willpower.

The waiter blinked a few times, as if removed from a trance, and smiled. "Here's your check, sir."

Jared's eyes scanned the check. He must've deceived so much that it was taking him a long time to calculate.

He handed Nick the check, pulling a twenty from his pocket. Nick checked the price for his food and fingered out seven dollars from his wallet. I searched my pockets for the only money I had left, but Jared placed his hand on mine. "It's okay, Cupid. I'll pay."

I tried not to blush. "No, it's all right. Let me pay for it."

"I said I got it."

"Aw, isn't that cute?" Nick laughed as Jared snatched the check from his hands. He handed it to the waiter before I had the chance to say anything and smiled that usual smug grin at me, slow and cool.

AS WE GOT IN THE car, I couldn't sit still in my seat. It wasn't out of boredom, but out of worry. I suddenly thought that all this worrying was getting a little overdramatic. To drown the thought from my head, I focused on Jared. He still had his arm extended securely around me. On the inside, I wasn't exactly sure if I trusted Nick and Demonica (well, definitely not Demonica), but I clung to the thought that Jared knew what he was doing.

I moved a little closer to him just to get a small touch of his warmth. We'd been driving for two hours now, and the temperature was gradually decreasing. I was wearing a sweatshirt, but I should've worn a jacket.

I gazed out the window, like I had been doing for hours. Trees and bushes seemed to whizz past us as we drove down the seemingly empty one-way road.

I felt Jared's hand rest on mine and I turned to face him. The soft look in his eyes melted my heart in a matter of seconds. He leaned in and whispered in my ear. "We're going to find a way out of this. But don't think about it too much. I just want this to be about you and me. Nothing else matters."

His deep eyes, fiery and powerful, watched mine. They burned into my heart, seeing through my soul. He closed the space between us, and I brought myself closer without realizing it. I could feel his heartbeat, steady and unbroken, keeping time with mine. His mouth brushed against my bottom lip. I closed my eyes.

But as soon as the moment came, it shattered.

"Breaker, breaker," Nick interrupted, mimicking the voice of a truck driver. "We've got a long day ahead of us on Route Love." He held a pair of sunglasses to his mouth like a radio.

"Hey! Give me those!" Demonica snatched back her glasses, wiping them on her shirt.

I suddenly remembered the situation we were in. "Really, Nick?"

Demonica butted in. "I don't think you realize it, but we're being tailed." She pointed out the back window.

I followed her gesture—and my heart lurched. A black car was in the same lane as ours—the same car I had been kidnapped in. I immediately tore my gaze away from the window to avoid suspicion.

"This isn't good." Jared continued to watch the car from the rearview mirror.

"Maybe they're just some random people." My reassuring words did nothing against my defensive instincts.

"I doubt it," Nick said, pressing the gas a little harder.

Demonica stopped him. "Don't do anything suspicious."

I noticed a turn coming up at the next light. "Make a right. Let's see if he's going to follow us."

Nick did as I said, but the car did the same. Jared swore.

"Okay, okay, okay," I said, feeling my panic rising. "Let's stay calm and think our way out of this." I risked another glance at the car. Black streaked the edges of my vision.

How had they found us? How had they known we would take this road? I had *known* we were going to be caught by surveillance. There didn't seem to be any plausible route of escape from the tension, nor from the situation. If we were caught, that would be the end of everything.

I hadn't realized just how fragile the task was until now, and when I did, everything around me that had seemed under firm control seemed to shatter into a thousand shards of glass. This wasn't some kind of movie where I could stay in my comfort zone without any doubts or worries. Now it was either life or death, truth or denial. Would we find a way to escape everything that posed a threat, or would we die trying to find a path to a hope that never existed?

"He's gaining on us. We have to step on it," Nick breathed, glaring into the rearview mirror.

"No! Don't do anything. They might have backup, and we'll be outnumbered," Demonica protested. For the first time, I saw a concerned look in her eyes, but the situation blocked out all vengeful feeling.

"Then what do you want me to do?" Nick fired back.

A thought struck me as if I were hit by lightning. "Haven't you two been through this before? Shouldn't you know what to do?"

"We *have* been through this before. Lots of times. But it takes time and thinking to escape out of traps like this," Nick replied. I knew he was trying to sound reassuring, but his tone said otherwise. "Relax. We got this."

"Make another turn at the next light." Demonica pointed to another intersection.

We slowed down at the turn before Nick made the left. I glanced at the car as it continued forward.

I sighed, relief rushing through me.

BY THE TIME NIGHT FELL, Nick had found his way back to the route we had been on, but he did something I wasn't expecting. The car bounced up to a plaza, with shacks and old stores, and parked the car in a tight space to avoid giving ourselves away.

"Why did we stop?" I asked, giving the streets a nervous glare.

"Do you have any weapons on you?" Nick asked.

"No."

"That's why we're here."

I blinked. "Um ... I've never touched a handgun before. I wouldn't know how to use one."

Nick turned to Demonica. "That's why you're coming with me."

"Why me?" The tone in her voice indicated she didn't want to get up.

"You're the one who knows about weapons the best; you can help me find a weapon that even untrained people can use." He turned back to Jared and me. "You two stay in the car. We can't afford having anyone see your faces."

Jared grimaced. Obviously, he needed to get out, but we

needed to stay hidden. After that incident with the black vehicle, we needed to keep our heads down a lot more often.

As soon as Nick and Demonica left, Jared leaned over to me, his eyes filled with desire. "Finally, we have some privacy."

"I'm just wondering if I could trust you in here. Dark ... alone ..." My fingers traced the rough muscles under his shirt. Jared's hands slowly clasped my head, and his thumbs circled my cheekbones in soft, intimate strokes.

All tension twisting my joints melted away, and I was falling into a secret world that belonged to us alone. One touch and I could clearly see Jared held the key to the lock of my heart, my soul.

"I think it's time we finished what we started earlier." Jared whispered, his lips softly brushing mine. I ran my fingers through his hair. Jared's mouth moved to my neck, where he planted warm kisses before nuzzling his head beneath my chin.

Jared's hand clasped mine, and when he let go, something rested on my palm. I carefully plucked up the gold-laced necklace with a black feather attached.

"This feather is special. It belongs to one of my wings, and it didn't die off like the others when I fell from the fight with the jets earlier." Jared clipped the necklace around my neck. "I can trust you with one of my feathers, with my life. Will you trust me with yours?"

I felt the feather's bristles lightly brushing my skin, as if it was alive, wanting to protect me, to love me, so much like Jared.

Our foreheads lightly touched, and I gazed deep into his

eyes, pushing meaning and resolve into my voice. "I will, Jared. I always have."

Jared leaned me back against the seat in a slow arc and bent over me. His black wings unfurled from his back.

In one swift movement, Jared's lips were pressed against mine, and a hot, electrifying sensation ran through my body. I wrapped my arms around his neck, drowning in his taste while he cradled my waist. Jared's mouth seemed to dance with mine, leaving me wanting more, and I sank deeper and deeper into him.

His hands roved up and down my arms, hastily exploring my skin before moving under my shirt and caressing my small stomach. I slipped my hands against his torso, feeling the muscles that tensed with silent heat under his skin.

The door swung open.

In a split second, Jared moved back.

Nick hastily reentered the car. His eyes were on the wheel. He gave us a glance, turned away, and looked back at us. "Uh ... am I disturbing anyone?"

Demonica slumped in the passenger seat.

"No. Let's get this show on the road," Jared said quickly. I was just glad that Demonica wasn't the one who had bothered us.

Nick shut the car door and turned around in the seat. I could see he had something tucked under his belt. He pulled out a switchblade. "Since you're the only one who's human," he started, seriously, "you need to keep a weapon close to you.

These people don't play around, and they *will* shoot anyone who looks suspicious to them."

"Thanks for the uplifting info," I said with a frown.

With a flick of his wrist, the switchblade unlocked. The silver razorblade edge reflected the light of the moon. He flicked it locked and handed it to me. "If anyone suspicious walks up to you, stab them and run. But keep it under your belt when you're not using it."

I inspected the weapon before tucking it safely behind my belt.

"Can we leave now?" Demonica asked, her cheek propped in her hand in boredom.

"Fine." Nick stuck the keys in the ignition and set the gear into drive. "Let's go."

Nick pulled out of the parking lot and steered back to the road.

As we entered the route to take the main highway, I felt sleep's taunting claws pulling me into a dream of black-and-white images I didn't understand. Jared's feather seemed to snuggle in deeper. I fingered the soft quill as the bristles brushed my skin in a warm, luxurious caress.

I gazed up at Jared, his face illuminated by each streetlight that passed, outlining his features.

His hand resting on mine was the last thing I felt before falling into a seemingly never-ending dream, not knowing what sweet nightmares lay ahead.

Chapter 8

PURSUIT

I thought told you to add ice with it!" my dad shouted at me, holding the glass to my face and spilling some of the water on the floor.

I jolted at his sudden aggressiveness and sniffled, wiping away the falling tears with the back of my sleeves. "I'm sorry, Daddy. I was helping Mommy wash the dishes, so I couldn't remember what you told me."

My dad's features seemed to harden in anger, and he threw the water in my face. "What have I told you about excuses?"

I held back the tears burning in my throat as cold water sprinkled my quivering bottom lip.

"Answer me when I talk to you!" he shouted, making me jump.

I sobbed. "That I'm supposed to do what you say."

He pointed a finger at me. "Exactly. As long as you live in this house, you are my property." He shoved the glass back into my hands. "Now go get me a glass of water with ice. And do it right this time."

"But you've been on the couch all day," I blurted. "Me and mommy have been working. Why can't you get up and get it? I'm tired and my feet are hurting."

Big mistake.

My dad drew his hand back, and I knew what was coming. He gave me a clean slap across my face. My cheek burned from the repercussion.

"What did you say just now, you useless piece of crap? Don't you ever tell me what to do!" he roared. "Do you understand?"

Frightened by what he might do next, I dropped the glass and ran to my room, slamming the door shut. The lock never really worked. I heard my dad storm after me and I hid myself in the closet. I saw my dad's shadow move into the doorway before he barged into the room.

I cringed, ready for anything.

I was always told never to back-talk, but this time, anger overwhelmed me, which was never a good thing to do around my dad.

Another set of footsteps hurried into the room, and I heard my mom's sweet, protective voice. "Babe, what's wrong?"

I peered through the gap in the closet door to see them arguing. My dad was shifting through the slightly damaged furniture in my room, pushing things aside, looking for me, while my mom stood in the doorway.

"'What's wrong?'" my dad fired back, his breathing heavy and labored. "That child doesn't know how to do crap! She can't even fill up a glass of water!"

"You can't blame her. She's been working all day. Give her a rest," my mom softly argued. "Here, relax. I'll get you a glass of water with ice."

I heard my dad stammering and sputtering, trying to grasp words to fight back but finding none. Giving up, he stomped out of the room. I saw my mom move towards the closet, and I tucked my head between my knees.

"It's okay, Destiny. Come out. He's gone," I heard my mom whisper in a reassuring tone. The sound of her voice always put my tension to rest.

Still whimpering and sobbing, I opened the closet door just a little to see my mom smiling reassuringly with compassionate eyes. I crawled out of my hiding space and threw my arms around her.

My mom carried me to the bed but didn't let me go. The tone of her voice was comforting but quickly became stern. "I've had it up to here with him."

Hot tears escaped my eyes and rolled down my cheek. I felt warm and safe next to her. She kissed my forehead and rocked me in her arms. The cold chill that gripped my heart melted away into a soft liquescence.

She wiped the tears away from my face, but more seeped out of my eyes.

"Daddy doesn't love me," I concluded. "He tells me to work, and he doesn't like what I do." I couldn't even remember the last time he said he loved me. I felt like I was living my life through the eyes of someone I didn't even know but grew to hate eventually, trapped in a world where everything that brought me pain was attracted to me like a magnet.

"I still love you," my mom covered up quickly. "Remember that, Destiny. I'll always love you, and that's never going to change. But one day, I'm not going to be here anymore." Her eyes stared off into the distance, as if trying to find something. "And you're going to have to fend for yourself."

There was something foreign in her voice whenever she spoke, and I couldn't ever put my finger on it. Her tone brought to mind an angelic tiger, protective but fierce. She wanted nothing but to protect me, and I never understood why she would even stay with my dad.

"But you're still going to love me?" I asked.

"Always."

I DISTINCTLY HEARD INCREASING WHISPERS in the front seats as I slowly awoke. My arms and legs felt like jelly, tired and frail, and I fought the urge to fall back into the never-ending trench of sleep. My mind caught distinct memories from the dream. I had promised myself I would never return to those horrible memories. The flashbacks seemed foggy and colorless, sometimes even with a dark, reluctant atmosphere.

I was nothing but a prisoner guarded by his raging abuse—

always had been, always would be. After my mom passed, I knew things couldn't get any worse. Once I turned sixteen and was allowed to leave the house sometimes, I spent my free time with my friends. But as the years passed, I grew increasingly rebellious against my dad. He threatened that I would never be able to go out ever again, but I never listened to him.

Now, running with Jared, I actually felt safer, knowing he loved me as I loved every single inch of his existence. I loved his voice, I loved the warmth of his body pressed up against mine, but mostly I loved the fact that he would fall for me despite our opposing species.

The whispers grew louder until I could tell there was an argument threatening to burst out. I shoved the memories that I'd had enough of out of my mind and focused on the next situation that dared to face us.

I glanced next to me to see Jared fully awake and joining in with the discussion. Unlike Nick and Demonica, streaks of worry were engraved in his features, and I instantly knew we were facing another problem.

I assumed the air outside was chilly, because mist painted the windows, silhouetting the trees and bushes outside. The sky was still dark, so I assumed it was around five in the morning.

My brain was still functioning slowly and my eyelids threatened to close, lulling me back into sleep. Rubbing my eyes wearily, I muttered, "Something wrong?"

At the sound of my voice, Jared threw me an anxious gaze. I could tell by the look in his eyes that something definitely was.

"It's nothing, Cupid," he lied, trying to keep me calm. Whatever the situation was, I knew it wasn't good. But I was a curious girl. I had to find out what was going on.

I leaned to the front and asked Nick. "Nick, what's going on?"

"It's okay. Don't worry about it."

I turned to Demonica. "Mind telling me what the problem is?"

Demonica gave it to me straight. "The main road to get to LA is crawling with police and SWAT teams, and there's a huge block. There's another way, but we'll come across police scattered around."

"Did you really have to tell her?" Nick barked.

"If we take the main road, we might be able to get through the block and not have to encounter any more investigators. If we take the second road, we'll have to deal with police the rest of the way, but not a lot."

I let this sink in. Which was better—having everything blown at you instantaneously in a matter of seconds or going through it, little by little, over a span of hours? Both choices balanced the scale, making the decision seem impossible to make.

"Look." Nick tried to claim the solution as his own. "If we can take the main road, we can get through the police, no questions asked."

"But the block is way too long of a wait. We'll never make it in time," Jared argued.

"Who said we were in a rush?"

"Can't we just deceive the officer who comes to our car?" I

asked. "The windows are tinted and they can't see clearly in the back. It's also still early in the morning. Jared and I will look the other way and pretend to sleep. Just tell them that we're traveling and tired."

A long pause settled over the car. The dead silence was palpable.

"Fine," Nick said at last, breaking the silence. "We'll take the main road. But don't come crying to me when this plan gets bombed."

Jared looked like he had just been intending to go with the plan chosen. Demonica looked slightly satisfied, but I could tell that she had wanted to convince Nick to go. I still felt a little tired and regularly dozed off into light stages of sleep. I gazed out the car window and saw that the sky still had that dark shade of blue and black, the stars slowly disappearing one by one. The pine trees lining the road towered too high for me to see the moon. It was still early, so maybe we would be able to slip past the police with little to no suspicion. Maybe.

I felt sleep crawling under my skin again, and I realized that though I might need the rest, I wouldn't be able to achieve it. I wanted so much to roll my eyes back and sleep, but at the same time, adrenaline kept me wide-awake, and I didn't want to accidently fall back into the dreams of when I was a little girl.

By the time we rounded onto the traffic-jammed streets, I could tell we were nearing the block. Most cars were being detoured, and officers were checking drivers and passengers, but Jared could easily deceive them.

My rising hopes soon descended when I heard Nick say, "That's not good."

I leaned to the front a bit more. "What's not good?" I answered my own question when I saw that the officers were wearing helmets and masks laced with wires and cables I was sure were packed with technology. I quickly ordered Nick to make a U-turn, but then I realized that would make us look suspicious. Plus, with the many cars crowding us, the task seemed impossible.

Ticking seconds stretched into minutes, and the officers were slowly making their way to us. We were so close to freedom, but punishment was moving faster. Our whispered discussion erupted into arguing. None of us knew what to do, making the situation seem to grow in size.

An officer with a radio headset halted at a car in front of us, cradling a clipboard and pen in his hands.

I eyed the doors, but we couldn't leave the car. Other vehicles were lining up in back of us, and there was no U-turn. We had to do something—anything.

As the officer made his way to our car, Jared swiftly pulled his hood over his head and rested against me. I hid my face in his muscular build and eased my breathing, making our "sleep" seem more believable. Jared's feather necklace felt soft against my skin, humming with that familiar sensation of desire.

I heard the officer knock on the closed window, and Nick rolled it down. I prayed he couldn't see Jared's wings.

"License?" the officer asked, as if he'd asked it a hundred

times. I could tell they'd been checking cars for hours. All night, probably.

"Sure," Nick said quickly to avoid the officer's eyes wandering to the back, where he would surely spot Jared's wings.

I risked a glance at the front seat, where the officer snatched Nick driver's license out of his hands. Clearly, he was in a bad mood.

After a few agonizing seconds of tension, the officer finally announced, "All right. You can pass—" He froze suddenly and beamed a flashlight in the darkness of backseat, magnifying Jared's wings. Our irises grew thin in the vibrant light.

"What the—?"

Nick stomped the gas.

The sudden movement of the Honda made me lunge in my seat, and I realized I hadn't fastened my seatbelt—another habit I would apparently have to break if we were going to start sudden car chases like this.

Nick sharply yanked the wheel to the left, driving in the grass to avoid hitting the cars in front of us. The Honda sped along, leaving behind a trail of dirt from the wheels. I glanced in the back window to see an array of officers scurrying into their vehicles and following the path we had taken. Red and blue lights flashed, and sirens wailed, making the scene look like something taken from a movie.

As soon as the traffic gave way to an open highway, Nick swerved back on the road. The Honda bumped over the pavement and onto the streets, and it was a miracle we didn't get a flat tire.

I could feel the cops gaining on us, and Nick pressed the gas further, dodging cars and vehicles in stubborn attempts to shake them off.

City life began to come into view, and we soon had the element of hiding between alleyways and parking lots.

Two extra police cars, which I assumed were backup, swerved around a corner ahead of us. Nick flung his foot on the brake, heaving the Honda to a complete stop. Throwing the gear into reverse, he took a street next to us, simultaneously avoiding the cop cars.

The road we'd taken apparently didn't have police security at all. Using this to our advantage, Nick backed the Honda into a dark alleyway. He and Jared jumped out and grabbed a large Dumpster with unbelievable strength. They hauled it in front of the Honda, hiding it from view as police cars sped past us.

My breathing was heavy and awkward. I was still slouched in my seat when Jared slumped back in the car. He seemed to be out of breath as well, but it didn't look like he was tired from moving the Dumpster.

A small smile crept up to his mouth. "Told you we'd get out of there." He pressed a kiss to my lips.

I managed to smile, but my heart was still pounding, and my pulse raced with adrenaline.

Demonica couldn't handle the heat in the back and threw herself out the door.

"If she hates me so much, why would you even bother calling her?" I asked.

Jared grimaced. "Believe me, it was never a willing trade. I called a few friends that other night in the hotel, but only Nick answered. He said that he'd help us, but he'd have to take his girlfriend with him."

Well, that explained a lot.

I heard Nick's low voice from outside the car. "Welcome to LA, guys."

Ever since we had entered the busy streets, I had known we were here. I was just too shocked at what was happening to care. I followed Jared out of the car, peered around the Dumpster, and gave the crowd-infested streets a long, fascinated look.

Street signs and billboards gave the streets and buildings a festive atmosphere as party spotlights danced in the early morning skies, which were still dark. The roads and sidewalks were packed with pedestrians, creating a scene that matched the thumping music coming from active clubs in the background.

The scent of cigarettes and alcohol floated out from a nearby bar, and I let out a few coughs from the smell. The air was freezing cold, buildings were lit with neon lights, and I instantly knew this would definitely be the place for Crystal.

I snuggled deeper in sweatshirt, wishing I'd taken something heavier with me. I turned back to Nick, my breath visible in the air, and I saw him popping open the trunk. He came back with a black Guess jacket with a lingering scent of expensive perfume. I assumed it was Demonica's, but I couldn't care less.

"All right," Nick said, double-locking the Honda. "It's best that we get a head start right now, while the sky is still dark. Everyone, stay in touch through your minds, and stay near the crowds of other dark angels. Don't get too close to high levels of technology, or else humans will see your wings."

Nick turned to me. "I'll take Destiny with me. We can't risk having the cops and investigators seeing you two together.

"We'll take the northern part of downtown. Jared and Demonica will take the southern area. If you manage to catch a dark angel, alert us, and we'll get there as soon as possible." Nick's eyes were darkened with something that looked like willpower.

We were finally here, but the sheer confidence I thought would come instinctively was missing. I wasn't sure I would be able to do this, but then again, I wasn't alone. I felt the slightest temptation to give up, but I crushed it. We'd come this far—we couldn't back down. I wanted to escape this, living every moment like I was about to die.

Nick's voice carried me back to reality. "Good luck."

Chapter 9

JUSTICE

Nick easily indicated who was human, who was fallen, and who was dark in the packed crowds of LA.

I didn't exactly like the place.

New faces that stared at me, music that I'd never even heard of, and the smell of liquor surrounded me, and traffic-jammed streets constantly protested with beeping car horns.

It was too dark to see what was ahead of us, but Nick seemed to have no problem with it. He darted and zipped in a crouch through the tight crowd of bodies, and I had to grasp his arm to keep up with him.

But there one particular thought was running through my mind. I wondered how we were going to catch this dark angel. We needed to find one that was isolated from the rest, but what if we were caught on surveillance? I was guessing that would make a great YouTube video: "Fallen Angel and Human Ambush Dark Angel."

But if we were caught, that would be the end of it. We were separated from our team, making it easier to get chased right into a dead end.

Part of me wanted none of this to be happening. Part of me wanted every second of it. If I had never saved Jared from those fighter jets and choppers because of my heart's stupid commands, I would have continued to live my life—but be stuck in it with an abusive father. I had made my choice, but something about it wasn't right, and I couldn't put my finger on it.

To distract me, I glanced at my watch. It read three thirty a.m.

"I see one heading inside that bar, and it's packed with humans!" Nick shouted to me over the loud uproar of chatter. "Here's our chance. Ready?"

I gulped down the panic and filled my lungs with air, taking on a firm expression. Even so, I was still panicking on the inside. I'd never fought a dark angel before, so this was new to me, which was a bad thing. I'd be better off if Jared was at my side, but that wasn't a possibility right now.

We followed the dark angel into the dimly lit bar, making ourselves look casual as we sauntered inside, our hands in our pockets. Red lights illuminated the interior of the bar, and a radio station I'd never listened to played low in the background, along with the sound of a TV airing a soccer game. The long table encased by chairs was busy with people as the bartender hurriedly mixed drinks and took orders.

Nick leaned in and spoke into my ear so no one else would hear. "Stand by the door leading to the kitchen. When the angel and I start fighting, open the kitchen door and follow me in."

I nodded in understanding.

My gaze was focused on Nick as he made his way to the dark angel, who was sitting hunched over the bar with an ice-cold beer glass. Nick tapped on his shoulder and sat next to him, before uttering something incomprehensible. The dark angel's dumbfounded expression told me it wasn't something good.

The dark angel suddenly shot up from his seat, his shoulders rising and falling with labored breathing and his hard-bitten features turning red in frustration. I could faintly see black searing the outline of his wings from the anger. I gestured for Nick to hurry up, but Nick held up one finger at me.

He picked up the beer glass and threw the alcohol on the dark angel's shirt.

The dark angel was infuriated.

As quick as a flash, he grabbed Nick by the scruff of his neck and flung him against the floor. I jolted in surprise, but Nick jumped right back up to his feet, seemingly unharmed. He hurdled himself at the dark angel's midsection, slamming him against the bar counter.

People from around the bar gathered around, gradually forming a circle around the two fighting angels. The bartender, on the other hand, just cleaned glasses and plates, as if he'd seen this every day. Wasn't he supposed to be calling the cops?

The crowd of people raised their fists in the air, mingling their voices in a constant, unbroken chant. "Fight! Fight! Fight!"

The scene reminded me of a moment in high school, when a group of about eighty students ran to the backside of Menchie's to witness a fight between two seniors. A video was posted to YouTube but was soon deleted, and the seniors and the student who posted the video were all suspended and held back a grade.

Nick landed several punches against the dark angel's jaw. The dark angel continued staggering back, unable to recover from any of the blows as Nick led him to the kitchen. I prepared myself as I threw the kitchen door open, revealing the narrow space. I was glad it was empty.

Nick thrust the bottom of his shoe against the dark angel's chest, throwing him inside.

I snatched a heavy steel pole from one of the sinks and held it over my shoulder, ready to swing in case he tried to attack me. I didn't know if he was drunk or sober, but it was best that I had something to defend myself with.

"You won't be needing that."

I whirled around as Nick locked the door and gazed at me with a sadistic grin, dark and easy. The dark angel jumped up from the floor and loomed over me as if he hadn't been just through a fight.

I was confused. "What's going on?"

"Good acting, Lucius," Nick said to the dark angel.

Lucius gave him a shadowy smile before gazing down at me. "So this is the girl? She's cute." His eyes grew sadistically aflame.

I backed away from him, but my back hit Nick, who was blocking the door. He ripped the pole away from me and held it out of my reach. I started piecing the puzzle together myself. "Nick, why?" This all had to have an explanation hiding behind it. Nick couldn't just betray me like that without reason.

"Don't try anything funny," Nick barked at Lucius, his tone thick with authority. "Our job was to knock her unconscious and take her to him."

"Yeah, yeah, I get it. Let's just get this over with." Lucius caught the steel pole midair as Nick tossed it to him, tapping it in his hand like a baseball bat.

I glanced around for a place to hide, but the "kitchen" was too narrow. It was no wonder Nick navigated his way to the bar so fast. They were planning to meet here to fake the fight and trap me inside.

I tried pushing past Nick, but he locked me in place. I tried calling out to Jared through my thoughts, but Nick used his own to block them before he deceived me into not moving. Nick used his mind to make my arms and legs feel like they were turned to stone. I couldn't move.

I ran through every plan in my thoughts but came up with nothing.

So my life was to end here? I had never finished my education. I had never traveled to Paris like I had said I would.

I couldn't live in abuse and have my life end before I could see the pleasures it had to offer me.

I squeezed my eyes shut, losing myself inside the false darkness. But I felt something vibrating with fiery, determined heat close to my chest. A soft burning sensation empowered me, seeming to escape from some hollow, cold corner of me and filter through every dark corner of the room. I could feel Jared's feather's warmth enclosing around my body.

Suddenly, Nick let out a pained cry and stumbled to his hands and knees. I was released from his deceiving.

Lucius grabbed the sides of his head, moaning, as if he had a terrible headache. He dropped the pole.

I had the smallest idea of snatching the pole and defending myself, but some unknown voice that spoke through me—or the feather—told me to get out of there.

I took their brief immobility to my advantage and threw myself out the door, which was now somehow unlocked.

THE HOTEL JARED AND I were staying at wasn't exactly fancy, but it was the closest one we could reach to hide.

Jared led me inside and carefully set me down on the bed. He seemed to take large notice of my body trembling in fear.

"He did *what*?" Jared exclaimed, pure vengeance engraving his features and voice. His gray eyes seemed to be set aflame with deep, burning anger, but I could sense a lingering trace of betrayal beneath them.

I wiped away a few tears that had leaked out of the corners

of my eyes. I had to admit I was scared. I had been assaulted before by Carlos Law, but coming so close to being kidnapped by a dark angel and a supposed friend in a bar was different.

It didn't look like Jared was trying to calm himself. His eyes were darkening, and venomous hatred vibrated under his skin and muscle. He clenched and unclenched his jaw before pulling me into a tight embrace. I buried my face in his jacket, letting the tears fall. It felt like Jared was the only person who can see me cry and not laugh, unlike my dad.

"How did you escape?" Jared asked, checking me over for the hundredth time to make sure I was all right.

I froze, remembering the way Jared's feather had increased in warmth, leaking out power that swirled around my body like a silk ribbon. I took off the feather necklace and studied it, wondering how it had helped carve my path of escape.

Jared fingered the black feather, before gazing at me, the retribution fading from his eyes. "I gave you the feather because I trusted you with my life. I loved you too much to let anything happen between us. If a human possesses an angel's feather, it can prevent him or her from certain harm. I couldn't trust anyone else to have one of my feathers. They might use it for ugly reasons."

On the inside, I could still see Jared as a guardian angel, despite his wing color.

Jared's eyes moved looked like he had something else on his mind. "Demonica also had a friend of hers try to ambush me in an alley. Good thing they had light poles near me to use as weapons."

"Why would they betray us like that?"

"To tell you the truth, Cupid, I have no idea. I've known them for years and can't see any reason why they would betray us."

"Do you know anyone else who might be behind this?"

Jared thought for a moment, and I was sure that he was thinking through the hundreds of people who wanted revenge against him. He replied, "Nope. Can't think of anyone."

So we had two fallen angel friends betray us out of the ordinary, we're *still* being chased by the government, and we're stuck in Los Angeles with no transportation. What path was there left to take?

"So what happens now?"

"Now, it's best that we wait until nightfall. Then we can go back out and find a dark angel's feather for celestial." Jared's eyes were burning with emotion that I knew wasn't composure. "And I don't care if anyone sees us or not. I won't let you out of my sight."

AT 10:00 P.M., JARED AND I prepared to go out.

I entered the bathroom and splashed cool water on my face to try to cool off. I hauled the towel off the sink hanger and buried my face in the white cloth, letting loose a sigh.

I stared at my reflection in the mirror for the first time in forever. Bags of worry and sleep deprivation had formed under my tired, weary eyes. I forced a smile, but it transformed my face into that of a complete stranger. I needed to find a way to get the old me back. After my mom's passing, Crystal had sculpted my personality, turning me into who I was. But Jared was all I had left.

I didn't know how long I had been staring at myself until Jared knocked on the door. "Ready, Cupid?"

I uttered a low sigh and sulked out the door before Jared stopped me. "I think there's something I should tell you." The lines engraved in his face told me he'd had trouble with this before. He took a deep breath and squeezed his eyes shut in a let's-get-this-over-with expression.

"Before we find the dark angel's feathers, there's something you need to know. If I sacrifice myself to become human, there's a high chance I will lose all memory of you *and* of being a dark angel."

I blinked, taking a moment to process what Jared had just said. If Jared became human, he'd forget all about me? I'd be reduced to a mere stranger in his new human eyes? It couldn't be. "Wait. So you're telling me that you're going to become human, but you won't remember me?"

"There's a small chance that won't happen," Jared said quickly.

"Oh, a *small* chance! It's uplifting to know that you won't even know my name when we're done with this!" I raised and lowered my arms in a sarcastic gesture.

"We can either have that battle-blood keep chasing us— me—or I take the chance of becoming human."

"Why didn't you tell me this before?"

"I wasn't sure you would agree with it. It might've been too much for you to take in."

Great. First Nick and Demonica, then Jared. I wasn't sure if I could even trust myself.

"Too much for me to ...? Jared, look at what's going on around us! If you expect me to be shocked at anything else, you're wrong."

"Destiny, I love you."

"But that's no reason for you to keep something this large from me. What else are you hiding? Did you even tell me the truth about your past?"

At that moment, stillness filled the tension in the air, and I was sure we could hear each other's heartbeats. Jared's dark eyes watched mine in silence, but the sentiment behind them was impossible to decode.

I held his gaze, not sure whether he was mad at me for questioning his past or sorrowful for keeping the truth out of my reach.

SPOTLIGHTS DANCED IN THE NIGHT sky, and the streets were a mass of cars and pedestrians, allowing Jared and me to fit right in. Even so, I kept a sharp eye out for Nick and Demonica, knowing that they were out there somewhere, probably looking for us.

I shivered in the cold air, snuggling deeper into Jared's jacket. We had decided to get rid of Demonica's jacket, as it might have a tracking device inside it. Plus, I was glad to throw it out. If it cost Demonica a fortune, getting rid of it would make it easier for her to see my daily pain.

I kept myself close to Jared, never loosening my grip on his hand, never allowing myself to draw my attention to something else. Jared wanted to find out what had encouraged Nick and Demonica to betray us, but we decided to find a dark angel's celestial wings first. But I had a fear of what they were hiding. One minute they were our allies, trustworthy, and the next, they were our enemies.

Everything mingled together only made me wonder what was to happen next.

I see one heading over there. Jared's alert voice resonated in my thoughts. With his mind touching mine, he indicated where the one he had seen was headed. A dark angel wearing a black leather jacket with a hood was heading away from the busy crowds and into an almost completely isolated area.

We followed him, hiding behind buildings and staying out of his line of vision. We watched him as he looked over his left shoulder and then his right and disappeared through the back door of a casino.

Should we go in? I asked Jared, suddenly afraid of entering strange places with biblical creatures.

No, there are too many immortals in there. You and I will stick out like a sore thumb. I'm going in and seeing if I can lure him outside. Wait here for me. If you see Nick or Demonica, run, and I'll find you later. We can't risk being seen with each other by the government, anyway.

Jared glanced up and down the streets, preparing to sprint off into the bar.

But to our surprise, the dark angel came bustling out with a fallen angel, fighting.

A gray hood was draped over the fallen angel's head, shadowing his face from view. He hurtled himself against the dark angel's stomach, ramming him against the wall. The dark angel's head slammed against the wall, before he shook himself to stay conscious. Rough black wings split from his back, and he charged at the fallen angel.

I gave Jared a questioning look, asking if we should leave and find another one.

But to my surprise, Jared was fixed with a dark glare as he watched the fight, clearly thinking.

Wait here was the last thought he sent me before running off to the private fight.

Lustrous, velvety, battle-hardened black wings burst from the seams of his back.

At first, I had no idea why Jared had just run off like that. We needed to retrieve dark angel wings and avoid fallen angels, not get ourselves into a fight between the two. But then I concluded that Jared was going to help the dark angel bring down the fallen angel, gaining his trust by doing so.

I watched as Jared's body flew a few feet above the ground and raced into the fight. The dark angel stumbled back in shock as Jared lashed out at the fallen angel with his fists.

Jared managed to land a solid hit against the fallen angel's nose, a river of blood following. The fallen angel fought in retaliation and confusion, aimlessly swinging his fists, disoriented.

Jared used his wings as a shield, blocking the attacks, as if pillows were being flung at him.

The fallen angel didn't sense the other dark angel creeping up behind him. He threw his arms lethally around the fallen angel's neck, jamming his airway shut.

The fallen angel clawed uselessly at the dark angel's arms, trying to free himself, but to no avail. The last image he saw was Jared's solid fist colliding with his face between the eyes.

The dark angel dropped the fallen angel's body before sending Jared a confused look. He muttered something I couldn't make out from this far away. Jared uttered a bark of laughter and replied with a tone of reassurance and affability.

I heard him speak into my thoughts. *Everything's clear. Come on.*

WALKING ALONGSIDE THE RIPPLING WATERS below the cement platform, Jared and I bonded with the dark angel. To make things more realistic, Jared deceived the dark angel into thinking that I was a fallen.

We decided it was best to lead the dark angel to the outer edge of the city and closer to the bay. Foam waves lapped against the jagged rocks that lined the cement platform. A cement pathway curved across the grass and around large sycamore trees tangled in vines.

We were far from any human or angel's view, but something told me this wasn't going to be easy. What if the dark angel fought back? Jared's sheer strength would lend us an advantage, but who knew how strong the dark angel was when using his full potential?

"So," I started, "I don't think I got your name."

A frisky aspect played on the dark angel's features. "What's yours?"

"Demonica," I lied.

"Liar."

I froze. Jared stopped in his tracks and stared at the dark angel, trying to decipher what he just said.

I blinked a few times and stammered, "Excuse me?"

"That's not your real name," the dark angel said, his mouth still tilted up in a playful motion, "Destiny Aubrey."

Before I could digest what was happening, the dark angel whipped his arm out against the air. Jared's eyes rolled up, his body going rigid.

The dark angel then grabbed me, holding me in place with his arm enclosed around my neckline.

In his other hand, he held a gun inches away from my head. I screamed.

Jared shook himself out of his trance and focused his eyes on me. I didn't know what the dark angel had done to him, but Jared had managed to endure it.

Jared's black wings burst from his back, but he stopped short when he glanced at the dark angel's face. His features distorted and shifted until someone else was holding me hostage—a familiar face that sent goose bumps down my spine, drowning me in aching irony.

Carlos Law stared at Jared in particular with a brutal grin.

"So it's come to this." He drew his black wings, his skin leathery but his feathers seemingly soft to the touch.

"You're a dark angel," Jared said. "That's a risky job working so close to the government."

Carlos continued to stare. His impatience seemed to vibrate under the surface of his wings. "You have no idea who I really am, do you? You've taken the most valuable thing from me. You've caused me so much pain."

"I've caused a lot of people pain. You'll have to be more specific."

Panic rose in my chest when Carlos pulled the gun closer to my head. "Don't you remember that night in the alley? You were still that weak girl's guardian angel. You took away my life."

I suddenly remembered the switchblade behind my belt.

I crept my hand to my jeans to reach for it, but not quick enough. Carlos reached it first, holding the gun and knife in one hand.

I then remembered Jared's feather necklace. Carlos disarmed me of that too. He hurled my only defenses into the water behind us.

"You killed the mortal I was supposed to protect," Jared said, his eyes blackened with venomous hatred that trembled under his skin. Ire and wrath were etched into his features. He curled his hands into fists. "It's your fault that I'm like this."

"A bit more of the opposite. *You* killed *me*. But when any angel kills a mortal, the mortal has a chance to come back. I returned as a dark angel, hunting for you day and night. I had

a life, and you destroyed it. Now I'm going to destroy yours."
He tilted back the hammer of the pistol.

"Stop!" Jared barked, backing away with his arms slightly
raised, meaning no harm. "Don't pull that trigger. Just ... what
do you want from me?"

I felt Carlos smile behind me. Clearly, he enjoyed seeing
Jared at his weakest. "I want you off the face of the earth. I
deceived your two fallen angel friends into leading you to LA
so I could finish you off myself. I separated you from your
girlfriend so I could attempt to take her hostage and reveal
myself to you. When that failed, I followed you until you saw
me go into that casino. I can't kill your body, but I can kill your
heart."

He lowered the gun to my arm, and fiery pain exploded
through my body.

It hurt too much to howl in agony.

The world around me spun, and every sound I heard was
muffled, as if I'd put on earmuffs. I felt like I was falling, but
my feet were still in place. I managed to interpret Jared's
screams of hurt and anger.

"I'll be waiting outside the abandoned Lady of LA church,
if you're interested," I heard Carlos say with a cold edge in his
voice.

I felt myself falling, falling, and ice-cold water struck my
body, drenching my clothes and hair. Seawater filled my
mouth, and when I tried to breathe in, water poured into my
lungs. Bubbles simmered across my vision, along with a red
liquid. Blood.

I knew we shouldn't have been so defenseless. Although I never knew much about dark angels, I should've known no one would just come walking right into our hands. Even so, we were running out of time and options.

The surface of the water blended out of my focus and I sank into the seemingly bottomless dark water. My vision danced in and out of attention, but I distinctly saw another body diving into the water, swimming after me.

I screamed Jared's name, over and over, but instead of words, a mass of empty bubbles fizzed before me.

I passed out before I knew it.

Chapter 10

TORN

I screamed. I kicked. I flailed my arms, but to no avail. My dad held me in a firm grip as we waited outside the operating room in a set of chairs lined up against the hallway. The blank white corridors smelled strongly of alcohol and sorrow.

Patients and doctors fixed me with disturbed stares, but I couldn't care less. Hot tears streamed down my face and I continued to call for my mom, whose life was hanging on the line somewhere behind the OR doors.

She'd been taken in for surgery on a stretcher hours ago, and I didn't understand why she hadn't come out yet. She had told me everything was going to be fine, but the longer I waited, the longer my searing doubts seemed to expand.

With every second that passed by, her words—even her voice—seemed to grow distant.

My patience seemed to hang by a thread, as did my fading confidence. Ideas that darkened my rushing thoughts locked my emotions in place. What if she didn't come back out? If she never made it through surgery, that would be the end of me—a piece taken from my already splintered heart, never to be replaced. I'd be a lone wolf, forced to live life in the worst way possible.

I struggled even harder and almost wriggled free of my dad's grasp, but he caught me again. I was seized by the desire to storm through the OR doors and look for her. He hissed in my ear. "Will you shut up, you idiotic piece of crap? People are staring at us."

"No!" I wailed, my breath catching. "I don't care! When's Mommy coming back?"

"Your mother is coming back when you shut your mouth. Don't make the same mistake you did in the car, Destiny." My dad squeezed my arm tighter in a threatening gesture. I whimpered at the memory of what he did to me in the car when I couldn't stop asking my mom where we were going and why she looked so pale.

I always hated that leather belt my dad wore.

When one of the surgeons emerged from the OR door, I froze. There was a small hint of reluctance in the lines in his face as he looked at my dad and then me. My dad clutched my arm tighter until it went red. He seethed into my ear. "If you move, I will make you bleed." He stood up and came face-to-face with the surgeon, telling him to give it to him straight.

I strained my ears to hear the conversation better.

"There's too much scar tissue clogging the veins leading to the heart. We've tried opening them up, but the cancer cells are eating the red and white blood cells even faster," the surgeon said, hesitant and sorrowful. "We're afraid to tell you that she might not make it. We'll have to take her off life support."

"And there's nothing you could do about it?" my dad asked suddenly. His breathing was normal, but his bagged eyes burned with a sizzling rage that could make anyone within ten feet of him shiver.

"Sir, I'm very sorry, but we don't have a cure, and the immune system is rapidly shutting down."

I took the risk and ignored my dad's warnings, sliding out of my chair. I gazed up at the surgeon, trying to squeeze out the last bit of hope. "Is my mommy going to be okay?"

The surgeon gazed at me before kneeling down to my level. "Sweetie, Mommy is very, very sick. We're working on her and doing everything we can to save her."

I swatted away a tear that rolled down my left cheek.

"But Mommy needs to rest and to get the rest she needs, she can't wake up."

A SMALL GROAN ESCAPED MY lips and my eyelids felt like heavy weights. The world around me spun even though my eyes were closed. Salt water drenched my hair and clothes, sending a shiver down my spine. Every square inch of me cried out in deliberate exhaustion.

I tried breathing in, but water gurgled in my lungs. Even though I was on land, I was drowning.

I managed to open my eyes, but everything was a blur, and my eyes were sticky. A familiar face leaned over mine, and I realized Jared was kneeling next to my body. I tried to say something, but the wrong words came out.

I knew Jared was next to me, but his muffled voice sounded thousands of miles away. "Destiny, can you hear me? Oh god, tell me you're breathing."

I licked my parched lips, trying to sit up in a shallow attempt at air, but my back only managed to lift off the ground a few inches before slumping back down.

I heard Jared giving me urgent orders through my thought channel. *Don't move, Destiny. Give it time. It'll work, okay? Just try to breathe.*

What'll work?

I felt a warm, almost velvety sensation spiraling in my chest and spreading throughout my body in a matrix of patterns. I shuddered as energy came rushing back, racing ferociously around me like smooth, searing fabric. The water filling my lungs began to disappear.

I instantly knew it was Jared's feather, healing me.

Within a matter of seconds, I gained enough strength to use my hands to push myself upright, coughing up leftover seawater. Disoriented, I fixed Jared with a long, terrified stare before throwing my arms around him.

I gave our surroundings a quick look. We were still in the area where Carlos had tricked us. The black seawater was lapping against the cement platform, encased by large, rough-surfaced rocks, and trees and brushwood were scattered behind us. At least we were alone.

"Carlos Law," I managed to stammer. "What happened?"

Jared's eyes grew dark, bloody revenge burning behind them. "He managed to get away. He threw you into the water, and I had to do something about it, so I dived in after you. He's going to make me meet him at the abandoned Lady of Los Angeles church, probably to lure me into a trap for your revenge, but I'm not falling for it. We need to leave."

"We need to—?" I stammered before staring at him with pure disbelief I was sure was etched into my features. "What do you mean we need to leave? What about Nick and Demonica? Carlos is deceiving them. We can't just leave him behind!" I tried to push him away from me, but the strength in my arms was still being restored.

"Destiny, I need to get you as far away from here as possible. With Carlos lurking around the city, you're as good as vulnerable."

"Can't you fight him?"

"I might die."

"But you're immortal."

"That doesn't mean he won't have some kind of advantage over me."

I opened my mouth to say something but then closed it. As much as I hated to admit it at the time, Jared was right.

If Carlos knew the most about dark angels, fallen angels, and celestial, killing Jared was merely a bump on his road for retribution.

"You don't know what we're up against here—" Jared continued before I stopped him again.

"But if we just keep running, who knows how long it'll be before we're caught? Nick and Demonica knew the most about the government, and if we get them back, they can help us the rest of the way."

It was Jared's turn to remain silent. His mouth formed a thin line, and his eyes locked mine in place. We both knew we were having the same thought throughout the long, tense silence.

I didn't want to be separated from Jared so early, but when the time came, I realized there wasn't much I could do about it, except talk Jared into doing what was needed to find Nick.

Despite all the car chases, fights, and betrayal, this grave moment right here, right now, was the darkest of all.

I was a curious girl, but I then realized my mistake. Curiosity was one thing that attracted danger.

I wanted to get the hell out of this place, but a part of me wanted to stay a little longer to find a way to save Nick. I didn't really care that much about Demonica, but she was Nick's girlfriend, and I knew it wouldn't be kindhearted to rescue him and leave her behind.

AN HOUR LATER, JARED FLEW us to a nearby hotel where I could stay while he attended the private meeting with Carlos.

My body was shaking, but it wasn't from the flight. It was my fear of Jared's death.

Jared set me down on the bed but never took his eyes off me. His dark eyes watched mine in silence as I took in every piece of him, trying to memorize all his details before he left, just in case he didn't come back.

Jared placed a warm hand on the side of my face, his thumb gently stroking my cheekbone in a soft, lavish sensation that caused my skin to electrify.

A low sigh escaped me. "You're coming back, right?"

Tears burned in the back of my eyes. I kept telling myself that nothing could possibly happen. Everything was just too perfect and innocent for any part of it to be destroyed by an opposing force that belonged only in nightmares.

Jared moved closer, and I could feel his warmth against my body like a furnace. "I can't make promises," he said in the most soothing, husky voice. "But I can let you know that I love you. Always have, always will. Remember that, Destiny."

The way he said my name caused my lower lip to tremble.

With his lips slightly parted, his mouth opened up under mine.

A hot, captivating sensation ran through my body and down to the tips of my toes. His mouth pressed against mine moved with a lattice of lust and desire. His hands progressed to my back with a searing sentiment that sent goose bumps scurrying across my skin.

He was mine. Every last inch from his mesmerizing eyes down to his bones was mine for the taking.

I closed my eyes, losing myself in a world where nothing mattered but him and me.

I caressed the edgy muscles on his arms, which were no one's but mine. I moved my hands over his torso, feeling the rippling muscle that trembled with aggravation under his skin.

Inhaling, I took in his scent of earth, roses, and mint.

Reluctantly, his lips parted from mine.

I held his gaze until he spoke. "You can still stay in touch with me through our minds. When I leave, I can send you mental images of what's going on and not get hurt."

I knew the look in my eyes gave him a response.

In one swift movement, he bent his forehead toward mine and closed his eyes. I felt a sudden shift in focus, and my senses blacked out for a fraction of a second.

Pulling away, Jared drew his black wings out, signaling that he was prepared for battle.

I watched him as he moved to the open window, spreading out his wings, which trembled with a velvety iridescence. They were sleek and lustrous and vibrated with an all-consuming black that seemed to swirl around me every time I looked.

He took one look back at me before his black wings slapped the air and he was gone.

So that was what a wife felt like when her soldier husband went to war.

Chapter 11

RIVALRY

By the time Jared landed behind the abandoned Lady of LA church, Carlos and Nick were waiting for him. His wings grew tight with broadness and rigidness, prepared for a fight, aware that I was watching the soon-to-be battle through his eyes.

A sadistically grinning moon crested above the sycamore trees that watched over the field of gravestones, painting the grass and tree branches with a silver glow. To the right, the abandoned church stood against the light of thriving city life, concealing them from anyone's view. To the left, a wrought-iron fence encased stone graves that were scattered across a gray, dreary cemetery that seemed to laugh with an ominous atmosphere, shrouded further by the heavy fog. A backdrop of shadowy green trees and brushwood darkened the graveyard setting.

Carlos was kneeling next to a grave, somewhat intrigued by the markings deeply etched into the gravestone's tough grit surface. Nick had his arms crossed over his chest; the smallest trace of enforced loyalty was frozen in his silent eyes. Carlos was deceiving him and Demonica, who'd been guiding Jared and me into a death trap.

Jared clenched his teeth, overcome by the need to snap Carlos's neck like a toothpick.

Carlos's head reeled up when he heard Jared's footsteps moving their way. His wings' relaxed posture tensed and then soothed. He fixed him with a violent smirk. "About time you showed up." He rose to his feet. "Come to avenge your girl?"

"She's safe," Jared said.

Carlos froze. Then, he returned to his usual cynical, dark attitude. "Well, that's a surprise."

Jared kept the conversation on track. "Where's Demonica?"

A sadistic smile was Carlos's only response.

Jared returned the look with a dark stare.

"If you managed to save your girlfriend, what are you doing here?" Carlos spoke out of conquest.

Jared stepped forward in a threatening gesture. "You know what I want." With a flick of his head, he gestured to Nick. "Release him, and I'll grant you approval to kill yourself after I'm through with you."

Carlos voiced a disbelieving bark of hard laughter, but the comedy was untraceable. Jared knew he couldn't kill Carlos;

no one could kill a dark angel. But if they became human, it was just the opposite.

"My tolerance is wearing thin with you, Carlos. This patience is like fire. You're not supposed to toy with it," Jared pushed on, coiling his hands into fists of stone. "Release him."

Carlos curled his fingers around his chin, pretending to be buried in thought. "Uh, let me think about that. How about ... no?" He turned to Nick and then back to Jared. "Beat him down."

Even though Carlos gave an order, Nick seemed to attack without warning. He swiftly lashed out with his fists, but Jared blocked each attack with a clean hurl of his arm.

Nick threw his right fist, but Jared caught it. His left went next, but Jared trapped that one as well.

Jared didn't see the foot coming. Nick thrust his boot against Jared's chest, knocking him back fifty feet. He crashed into a tree nestled beside the church, all the air knocked out of his lungs.

Jared shook his head to clear his doubled vision.

He didn't see Carlos standing where he was before. Jared made a crude, humorous assumption that he ran off like the frightened child he was, his tail between his legs.

Nick charged back at Jared with incredible speed. His features were so stiff that creased lines divided his eyebrows. Jared dived to the left, dodging the attack, and Nick slammed into the tree so hard that it vibrated before it cracked in half and tumbled to the ground.

Nick's fighting style seemed to contain larger amounts

of firepower, just as Carlos had designed it, but he was sloppy. Disadvantage was gleaming all over him; Carlos had just become a dark angel recently, so he didn't have much experience in supernatural combat or deceiving. Even so, he had the training of an FBI agent, so tricking Jared and me had been simple.

Nick swayed on his feet, dazed by the impact with the tree. Jared took advantage of his brief immobility. He grabbed Nick's wrists and pinned him in place against the outer wall of the church.

Then, staring directly into Nick's eyes, Jared focused on his thoughts, channeling them from his subconscious into full awareness. Gathering the thoughts and orders into one clump, he directed them at Nick, unleashing them at full mental power.

Nick's head trembled under pressure as he tried to barricade the aggressively attacking thoughts sent from Jared's mind. His eyes grew bloodshot. He tried to utter something, but the wrong words came out.

Jared felt around Nick's thoughts, trying to find the orders that Carlos had connected and pull the plug. He tightly gripped a certain thought with all his rational strength, for it was thrashing around wildly, sending unwanted thoughts throughout the networks.

Jared willed himself to grasp the thought, and he pulled out.

He literally stumbled back from the force it took to complete the job.

Nick's eyes rolled up and he sank to the floor, unconscious.

Breathing heavily, Jared glanced around the cemetery for Carlos, but his location was completely unknown. A small vindictive corner of Jared wanted to scream and curse Carlos's name in anger. Another part told him to grab Nick and get out of there. But he needed to find out where Carlos was hiding Demonica first. If he left, he might lose track of Carlos's location and thus Demonica's as well.

Against all odds, a flying silhouette was darting straight toward Jared. Carlos drove his right shoulder deep into Jared's midsection. He was holding a gleaming sword made of a transparent gold—celestial.

Carlos flung Jared at an angle against the ground below them. Jared's limp body plowed into the soft, grassy earth, leaving a trail of dirt and soil behind.

Jared dug his fingernails into the dirt to try to slow his body. He came to a slow halt beside a stone sculpture of an angel toppled over a half-sunken grave.

The angel statue gripped a long, sharp weapon in its right hand.

Jared grasped the hilt and pulled a rusty but durable sword out of the statue's grasp.

If Carlos wanted a fight, he was already dead to Jared.

He reeled his head to the sky to see Carlos dropping back down to the ground for another attack. Jared ran the other way, spreading his wings to prepare for flight. His wings beat the air, and the ground seemed to give way beneath him. He launched into the skies with Carlos following right behind.

Jared whirled around to face Carlos and continued fluttering his wings so that he was flying in reverse. He raised his sword to shoulder level just as Carlos came crashing into him.

Carlos's sights were set on Jared's black wings, trying to sever them off his back with the celestial blade, making him incapable of flight. But Jared held the speed that seemed faster than light itself.

Carlos launched his foot square in Jared's chest, hurling him against the outer wall of the abandoned church. Jared's back struck the stone, producing a layer of latticelike cracks on the wall.

Carlos came charging back at him, his wings spread over his back like a black blanket.

Jared relaxed his wings, letting himself fall and dodge the attack.

Carlos planted his feet against the wall of the church and pushed off, charging back at Jared, gaining more speed in the move. Carlos swung his celestial sword lethally at Jared's neck and wings, but Jared managed to fend off the attacks with several clean hurls of his own blade.

With each powerful lash and stroke of his sword, I knew Jared focused a small portion of his thoughts on me. If he didn't win this fight, we would both drown in defeat and death.

Knowing he needed to sever Carlos's wings for an advantage, Jared soared higher into the black sky, thumping his wings against the air to gain altitude. He glanced down to make sure Carlos was following. Everything was going according to plan, but something told Jared this wasn't going to be as easy as he thought.

A wave of alarm rippled through Jared's senses. Instantly, he knew something was wrong.

An icy sensation ran down his spine as he scanned his surroundings.

Something slammed into him from behind.

Instinctively, he regained his position and kept his sword ready to strike at Carlos. But something else stood before him—something that tore him between panic and rage.

The battle-blood lunged at Jared for another lethal attack, but Jared frisked to the side, and the shadow darted past him and lunged for Carlos next. Carlos raised his celestial sword and swung it down against the shadow with all his might.

The sword passed right through the battle-blood's form, as if it was made of air.

Realizing that the battle-blood could kill Carlos, Jared darted into the fight. He needed Carlos alive to retrieve Demonica's location.

Jared tensed his black wings and lunged at the battle-blood, beating his sword at the silhouette's body in a futile attempt to injure it or chase it off. Jared couldn't even touch the silhouette—but the silhouette could touch Jared.

The battle-blood whirled around to face Jared before it lashed a single arm, throwing him back fifty feet. Jared plowed into the ground far below them at the southern border of the graveyard.

The battle-blood then turned to face Carlos. He uselessly thrashed the blade of his sword against its body as it hurtled itself at him. It grabbed his black wings and began dragging him down from the black skies to the ground, which was now a hundred feet below them.

Carlos's black, battered wings began to shrivel before slowly deteriorating. Soon, the only things left of his wings were hollow, yellow bones.

Carlos thrashed against the silhouette, but his struggles were rendered useless when it threw him against the ground, flinging the soft, brown soil around him into the air. Carlos made an attempt to regain flight and battle the silhouette but he couldn't move. His mouth gaped open in shock as his skin began to diminish and blood dribbled down his forehead and nose.

Jared batted the grass out of his way as he ran to his enemy. Realizing Carlos was going to die, he shoved aside his seething thirst for vengeance and screamed, *"Where the hell is Demonica?"*

Instead of answering, Carlos uttered a noise that sounded like something was choking him from inside his throat.

A soaring noise shifted Jared's attention behind his back. The battle-blood charged at Jared, hovering a few feet above the ground. It slammed into Jared's ribcage and skyrocketed back into the black sky, dragging him with it.

Darkness encroached Jared's vision, making him unable to tell whether the night sky or the battle-blood's silhouette form was blinding him. He felt his wings vibrate violently before curling into a shriveled lump of black feathers.

His rapidly thrashing thoughts moved to mine. He instantly

knew that he failed and that he would drag me into certain death with him.

Jared managed to release himself from the battle-blood's grip, but as a result he fell to the ground far below them. He rapidly flailed what was left of his black wings, unsuccessfully trying to remain in the air.

The brown soil below them was hastily rushing up to meet him, and the wind screaming in his ears only quickened his rapid heartbeat. But the rush of the fall held no upper hand against his searing failure.

Cupid, I'm sorry. I told you that I wouldn't fail. I promised you that I would come back. I failed. And I never should have taken responsibility for keeping you with me.

Jared whirled his head back above him to see the battle-blood briskly flying down after him, narrowing its black, leathery wings to gain speed.

Darkness began to trace the edges of his vision with a slight lurking hue of purple. He couldn't even see the ground.

Destiny, go get the car and get out of here. I'm not coming back, but that doesn't mean I won't leave you. I—

A flicker of dim lights was the last thing he saw.

Chapter 12

AGONY

My heart beat against my ribs as I woke with a jolt. Disoriented, I felt around the ice-cold bedsheets for the familiar warmth of Jared's body heat, but my fingers grasped nothing.

I lay there, staring blankly at the ceiling above me, trying to process what I had just witnessed.

Something was stirring on my chest, and I jumped when I saw something small and black resting on my breastbone.

Jared's feather was curling up, black bristles falling off one by one, dying.

The colorless flashes of the memory came roaring back to me, too corrupt for me to digest. It had all happened way too fast.

Carlos didn't kill Jared like I thought he would. But having the silhouette find them and take them both took it to a whole different level.

I stopped my thoughts there. Jared wasn't gone. He couldn't be. I knew the reality was much more painful and that my thoughts were ridiculous, but I needed something—anything—to comfort me.

Jared was the only source of light in my dark world, a feeling of soft, warm emotion in my state of numbness, and a tone of color in my life of empty pages.

The illuminated space between us had died out, distancing us so much that it hurt to be breathing without him. It felt like a thousand shards of glass had been stuck under the surface of my beating heart.

Closing my eyes, I tried to regain the memories of Jared before they faded from my thoughts forever. I recalled his lingering smell of earth, mint, and spice. I reminisced on his laughter, smooth and strong. I remembered the way he touched me, the way he kissed me.

As I fingered his dead feather, I began to wonder about my future. I didn't know my way around this place, so what was I going to do if I ran into the government again? I doubted I would have an actual worthy fate, since Jared and the rest were gone.

Three solid raps sounded from the door.

I jumped at the sound, swinging my feet off the bed and looking through the eyehole.

Nick stood on the other side of the door, pacing the hallway with his hands buried in his pockets. His features contained lines of regret and shame, but he could've been faking it.

I leaned my back against the door, deciding not to let him know I was there.

Did Jared manage to free Nick of the deceiving? I had seen through the images that he had been knocked out promptly by the pain, but that didn't mean Carlos hadn't enhanced the trick into letting Nick betray us even when he was dead.

"Destiny. It's me. It's all right. You can open the door."

I remained silent.

"I saw what happened with Jared and the fight. Carlos's deceiving wore off when he was taken." Nick spoke with such composure, such assurance, that I was almost drawn to believe him.

I told myself that I needed to keep my guard up, but some sage part of me ordered me to let him inside. Biting my lip, I twisted the knob and cracked the door open just enough for me to see through.

I glanced down the hallway to make sure no one was with Nick and that he really had been released from deceiving. Carlos was dead, so his deceiving *had* to have worn off.

Opening the doors fully, I let Nick inside the room. He closed the door behind us, kneeled down to my level, and pulled me into a sorrowful embrace. I burst into tears.

The way Nick's eyes were at the moment he had trapped me with the dark angel were so different compared to now. Carlos had been controlling him the whole time, and I had told Jared I wanted to save him. *I* had forced Jared to fight Carlos. *I* had led him straight into the clutches of the silhouette. Jared's death was *my* fault.

It was all because of me.

I let out powerful, echoing cries of remorse, shame, and longing that came from a vessel deep within me, a vessel that erupted with grief and anger like almost never before. The only time I had ever felt this much pain was when Mom had passed from cancer.

I wanted Jared back—no, I *needed* him back. From the moment he had saved me from the government jets until we began running away together, I knew by the look in his eyes that we were meant to be much more than the typical teenager couple hanging around school.

Hot tears rolled down my cheeks as I squeezed my eyes shut, remembering the fire that burned in his eyes every time he touched me, every time he looked at me.

Jared, I thought. *Please come back.*

I SAT IN THE FRONT passenger seat of Nick's Honda Civic, watching the trees, bushes, and streetlights flash beyond window before rushing out of sight. The moon that sat rigid above the thick brushwood seemed to throw a fit of coarse laughter in my face, as if it were the cause of my misery.

I was missing the familiar warmth of Jared's hand clasped on mine. I was missing the way he held me. I was missing his voice, smooth and husky.

A knot formed in my throat as tears burned behind my eyes, but I forced them back.

Demonica had been released from her deceiving as soon as Carlos was taken by the silhouette. After what Carlos did to her, she needed some time alone. And I was thankful that she'd decided to drive a stolen car.

I crushed my palms into my eyes. How could we let something as terrible as this happen so effortlessly?

Nick tried lessening the heaviness in the air around us by turning on the radio. Breaking Benjamin was the first sound that came from the speakers. I turned it off.

Nick's iPhone chimed with a text. He unlocked the device to read it.

"It's Demonica. She wants to meet us somewhere to pick up food since we can't stop anywhere." Nick turned his attention to me, but I was in too much pain to give a response. "I'll text her back saying we're on our way. You'll wait in the car in the garage. You still can't be seen by anyone."

I was better off.

Chapter 13

ASSAULT

I waited in the car while Nick left to get the food. Since we were still running away and had just lost a teammate, we were probably going to have to eat while on the road.

Nick's Toyota was parked in the middle of the multistory garage. If we parked the car at a higher story and the government found us, we'd have a minor, unlikely chance of escaping through the exit downstairs. If we parked the car at a lower story and got caught, we'd be captured that much easier. We decided on something in between.

Just to torture myself, I stared out at the gray, motionless scenery of the garage beyond the window of the Honda, picturing Jared's features before they grew worn, faded, and weary from my remembrance. I remembered his feather's warmth. Even as I fingered his dead feather and knew he was gone forever, he still felt alive to me.

Closing my eyes, I created my own alternate universe, a universe where I had everything I ever wanted. I imagined that Jared was near me, holding me.

But those dreams had been broken.

I had had two options. One was to stay at home and continue to be beaten up by my abusive dad, and the other was to run away from it all with Jared at my side. Even though it was too late to change my decision, it seemed that no matter what I chose, it wouldn't matter. In the end, I would suffer.

As I drowned helplessly in my own inner agony, I barely noticed Nick running back to the car in alarm. He flung open the car door, threw himself in, and tightened the seatbelt on my chest and waist.

I stared at him. Another chase?

"I knew we shouldn't have traveled separately." Nick murmured as he stuck the keys in the ignition. His tone was somnolent with exhaustion, but his eyes darted with panic, which caught my attention, shattered or not.

I pressed my face to the window to see what he was going to run away from. My heart beat against my ribs when I got my answer. A vibrant spotlight beamed through the gaps in the parking garage, and from outside I could hear the sound of multiple helicopters' rotating blades.

Nick stomped the gas.

My heartbeat picked up speed as Nick raced through the tapered garage levels. I knew he was heading for the nearest lower exit to escape before they sent armored vehicles in. I then realized it was too late for that. Equipped vans and cars rolled in through every possible lower exit we could escape to. Nick finally hit the brakes and yanked the wheel to the right in his hurry, sending the car into a half tailspin before he fled upstairs.

I had split-second views of the troops and gunmen clinging to the sides of the vans as they followed us up the steep ramp that led to a higher level. They were wearing gas masks.

It only took me a moment to know why they needed them.

A white cloud of dense cotton vapor swept in through the gaps from the choppers outside. I heard Nick swear as the tear gas clogged our vision beyond the car's windshield. Thick fog wafted in through the AC vents.

"They're trying to smoke us out! I can't drive like this; we could crash. We need to run on foot," Nick said as he steered the car into a deserted part of the garage where no one would be able to see us. He stopped the car when the tear gas expelling from the AC vents spread halfway through the car. My eyes grew papery dry and itchy, as if cotton was being pressed to them, even after I closed them.

My mouth watered, and my lungs were on fire. I ground my hands into my eyes and clenched my teeth.

Disorientation gripped my thoughts, and I had a split-second view of Nick popping open the glove compartment. He produced a gun. With red and weary eyes, he shoved the firearm into my hands and pushed open the doors to get out. My seatbelt was jammed, but I managed to wrench it free.

I flung myself out of the car and followed Nick's silhouette through the heavy white gas. I coughed and gagged against it, feeling as if acid foam were rising in my throat. It was impossible to know whether I was running and actually going anywhere. The world around me looked like a white blanket had been thrown over my head, and I felt my body gravitating to the floor from the lack of focus.

I peered through the mist, trying to interpret Nick's figure as it gradually faded into the mist. I tripped and fell twice in failed attempts to catch up. It was when Nick's silhouette completely disappeared that I really started to panic.

"Nick?" I called in a hoarse, jagged tone. I was surprised by my own voice, which had been sucked dry by the tear gas. I held the pistol close to me as I heard footsteps running in from behind me. Looking back with blurred vision, I could barely decipher multiple gas-masked silhouettes emerging through the tear gas. I quickened my pace. I twisted around and aimlessly fired multiple bullets at the silhouettes, which was a huge mistake, since I couldn't allow them to know my location.

I continued running, calling Nick's name out through my thought channels. *Nick, I lost you! Where are you?*

Tears of panic and fear rolled down my cheeks as I waited for a response. I was about to call my own defeat, when miraculously, Nick answered. *Keep running, and don't let them see you. Find somewhere to hide and I'll find you.*

Coughing and wheezing from the gas, I nodded my head, even though we were talking through our minds.

Through my burning panic, I thought I noticed another group of gas-masked silhouettes just ahead of me. Swallowing down my own anxiety, I whirled around and checked the smoky area behind me, where the other troops sprinting my way. They had me trapped.

I acted on the first thought that sprung to my head. I crouched and made my way to the parked cars that lined the right side of the wide corridor. I hid myself in a stoop between a black Lexus SUV and the wall it was parked next to.

My vision began to darken as I peered around the large SUV tire at the troop's silhouettes moving through the fog, some taking cover, while others moved in to search for me. I made an attempt to hold the gun closer to me, but then I realized I dropped it somewhere in the gas.

Nick! Please answer me!

Nick gave no reply. I continued to call through my thought channels, but only the enduring hush of white noise was there to answer me. I knew right then that this was the end. Jared was gone. I was trapped with tear gas. I had nothing left.

I tried not to cough, giving away my hiding place, but the invisible flames that danced on my skin and inside my lungs were more than I could take. Throwing a hand over my mouth, I burst into a fit of coughing. The silhouettes whirled around to face the Lexus SUV I was hiding behind, slowing moving toward me.

I wanted to run, but my body refused to move. I wanted to scream, but my voice was gone. I didn't realize I was on the floor until I noticed Jared's dead feather lying inches away from my face, but everything was burning too much to feel the chill. I half-expected it to burst to life and envelop me in warmth and reassurance, clearing a path for me to escape.

Something darted across my line of vision.

Multiple troops fell on their backs as though knocked down.

Peering through the fog of confusion, I saw the man's shadow run at incredibly high speeds toward the soldiers once more. Attaining the ability to open fire at whoever was attacking them, they raised their weapons as sparks of light ruptured from the barrels of their guns. I stared at the man's silhouette against the white gas, expecting it to fall to the floor from the repercussion of the bullets.

If things weren't odd or confusing enough, I would've been surprised at the fact that the bullets reflected right off the surface of his form. After standing there as if nothing had hit him, he charged back at the soldiers, using his bare fists to knock their rifles clean out of their grasp.

In a matter of seconds, multiple bodies lay on the floor. The tear gas hanging in the air was a blend of white and red around the man's silhouette.

Nick? I asked him through my thought channels. But I knew it couldn't be him—he hadn't answered. I knew it couldn't be Jared either—he was dead, and moving bullets didn't have the ability to bounce off his flesh.

Panic rose in my chest when all I was able to see was darkness. Had I gone blind from the tear gas? The thought of it sent a fresh wave of horror crashing over me. I could hear many more footsteps thudding from both sides of the garage, and I knew that double the amount of troops had been sent in.

I felt someone's rigid hands grab me from behind, dragging me out of my hiding space. I struggled against the man, knowing for sure that he was one of the soldiers sent in after me. I tried to scream, but the only sound that escaped out of my mouth was a guttural whisper.

Tears streamed down my face.

So this was what the end felt like. My dad would get away with half a lifetime of abuse. The only person I had felt a strong emotion for in years was dead. And I was about to be taken into custody by the government, the death penalty gleaming all over me.

I threw away any hope of ever escaping and sank into unconsciousness.

I gave up.

Chapter 14

JUSTIFY

I regained consciousness but kept my eyes shut.

I had been found and dragged away by a soldier in the garage, but the tear gas had knocked me unconscious before I could witness what happened next. My first guess was that they had taken me to some sort of solitary criminal confinement where I was waiting interrogation. They were probably going to ask me questions about where Jared was hiding. I was well aware that I couldn't answer a question like that. He was dead.

I was lying on my back, and the sheets and mattress told me I was on a bed, probably inside a prison cell.

When I opened my eyes, the first thing that took color was

the dark-yellow ceiling. The lights were off and the air was cold, giving the room a dark, icy atmosphere.

I expected a burning, stinging sensation pricking at my eyes when I opened them, but to my surprise, they were … perfectly fine. It felt like waking up on a flawlessly normal day on my bed. The raw blotches on my skin were gone as well, as if they had been healed.

But that was impossible. I had just gone through an hour of a torturous tear gas assault. And Jared's feather had died along with him; it didn't work anymore. How could I not be feeling any pain?

Turning my head, I set my gaze over my left shoulder, and I saw a familiar face in the shadows. In the dark, his ashen eyes watched mine in silence.

Jared sat hunched over a chair, wearing only a pair of black skinny jeans.

My heart bumped against my ribs as I continued to throw long stares at him, trying to determine if Jared—someone I thought was long dead—was actually sitting next to the bed I was lying on. I tried blinking several times, expecting the image to dissipate from my vision.

But it didn't. It was real. Jared was alive, sitting right next to me. He had saved me from the troops inside the garage. It wasn't a soldier who had dragged me out from behind the SUV—it was Jared. He must've carried me out of the garage and found his way to a nearby hotel.

"Jared," I said in an unsteady whisper.

Jared's soft, powerful voice crawled through the darkness

in a whisper. "Shh. Don't speak. We need to keep a low profile for now." His eyes cautiously moved to the closed window. The streetlights illuminating the night spilled through the gaps in the shutters.

Questions circulated in my thoughts like a cyclone.

What had happened to the others? Where was Carlos? How had Jared survived?

What ... happened? I asked through our thought channels. Tears burned behind my eyes. I fought the urge to break down crying.

Jared let out an exhausted tuft of air from his nostrils. *When I fell from the sky, the battle-blood didn't take me. I didn't die. And neither did Carlos. I still had the bones from my wings, so I transferred them to Carlos so I could become one of the fallen.*

You did what?

Let me explain. If I fell, it meant the battle-blood couldn't touch me; they only go for the powerful ones—the ones with black wings. Carlos's wings were gone completely, so I gave mine to him. After that, I deceived him into running straight into the garage with me. At the time, I knew you and the others were surrounded by SWAT in the garage, so I deceived Carlos into distracting the soldiers. That gave me just enough time for me to go in and get you out.

What happened with the others? I asked.

We're staying in separate hotels. Carlos is still out there, and I'm deceiving him. Right now, he's distracting any government officials. He's showing them his face right in front of them. They never got a clear view of mine, so they'll think that Carlos is the dark angel they're searching for.

I pondered everything he was saying. Jared fell to stay away from the battle-blood, but he had to give Carlos his wings to do so. After that, he had deceived Carlos into attracting government attention, making him the prime suspect. So now Carlos was being chased by the government *and* the battle-blood. But there was still one hole left to fill.

What about me? I asked. *The government unintentionally left you out of the picture, but that doesn't change the fact that they'll continue to chase me—*

Jared cut me off. *They don't know who you are.*

I paused for a few counts, trying to allow what Jared had said to sink in, but the words wouldn't process.

Jared took notice of my mild shock. *Carlos was the only government agent who saw you with me. I questioned him. He was trying to fool you into thinking that the entire government agency was looking for you too. Remember that night at the back of the movie theater?*

Shivering at the memory of being handcuffed and thrown into the trunk of a car, I nodded.

Carlos hired a fallen angel to drive the car. They made you think that the government had its eyes on you so that you could run away with me. He knew we were going to LA to find celestial, so he planned everything out behind the scenes to get me right where he wanted me. And he brought you along with me so he could have someone's life to threaten.

So ... I was never a prime suspect? I pushed disbelief behind the words. But this was a dark angel we were messing with. If it came to immortals, I knew I was in for many more unimaginable circumstances—circumstances so inconceivable, they were powerful enough to use the government as a ragdoll, a puppet to be used before thrown out of the picture for personal business.

Jared shook his head. *Carlos led us to believe that you were. Now that I've fallen, the battle-blood will stop chasing us, but that doesn't mean this is over. My deceiving on Carlos won't last forever, so he'll come to his senses sooner or later. He'll know what I've done, and there's no undoing it. He'll want revenge, and he won't stop until he gets it. Until we find a way to kill him, or at least get the battle-blood to take him, we need to keep ourselves on high alert.*

I didn't realize I was holding my breath until Jared leaned over me, something pained and sorrowful moving in his eyes. I noticed that some sort of red liquid trickled down his back before landing on the white sheets like crimson tears.

Driven by concern, I cast a glance at where his wings had once been fused and instead saw two fresh scars that ran down the length of his back. White broken bone that had once connected to his black wings poked out from the red, raw, open wounds.

Something in my chest fluttered in pain at the sight. Even though he wasn't able to feel pain, I felt it, fighting the urge to cry.

Before I could stop myself or even know what I was going to do, I threw my arms around his neck, drew him close, and kissed him. My mouth took shape around his as I kissed him harder.

Jared's arms wrapped around me, holding me against him. The familiar warmth of his body heat and the distinct scent of earth and herb told me the moment was real. Every taste, every scent, every sensation I had thought was lost forever was now right here, drowning me with anything and everything that I ever could have wanted.

Jared slowly pulled away, only to nuzzle my neck.

I fluttered my hands through his hair and then down his torso, tracing my fingers along his jawline and the rippling muscles of his arms, making sure that everything was real and not some lie created by the power of my dreams.

I sank deeper into Jared, wanting nothing more than to feel him near me, warm, real, alive.

Then I felt it—that familiar, warm, fuzzy sensation that filled me with heartened hope and burned to my core with powerful affection. I set my gaze on Jared's black feather necklace, now bursting with fiery life. The black bristles snuggled into my bare skin through my V-neck.

But Jared's feather had died—I had seen it.

Your feather! I blurted. *How ...?*

Once I gave Carlos my wings, I kept one of the feathers that were still alive. I knew the old one was dead, so I saved a new one for you. I burned the old feather. We couldn't risk having two of them; if we lost one and someone else found it ...

His thoughts' voice trailed off, and I understood that the repercussion of someone finding his feather would be lethal.

In the corner of my eye, a spotlight slowly swept across the window from outside and seeped through the gaps of the closed shutters. Jared swiftly climbed off the bed and hid behind it. I kept my head down. Neither of us made a noise.

The spotlight moved away from the window, and I heard the chopper's spinning blades fade away into the distance. The relief of the tension felt like a pile of bricks was lifted from my chest.

What are we going to do now? I asked, swallowing down the lingering panic that clogged my throat.

Once all the commotion dies down, I'm dropping you back home. Running for the rest of your life from the government like this isn't a moral way to live, even though you have a stupid father.

Despite my need to be as far away from my dad as possible, Jared was right. I couldn't continue to run away from the government until the day I died. There was a path ready to lead me back home—to a life as close as possible to *normal.*

After pondering everything Jared had told me, I reluctantly came to a decision.

"All right," I breathed. "Crystal is probably waiting for me. Let's hope she didn't leave my purse at the theater."

EPILOGUE

Napa, California
January 5
Five months later

Brushing my hand over the line of books, I stopped when I took notice of a black, leather-bound novel. Golden calligraphy letters were etched into the spine of the cover.

Removing the paperback from where it sat, I quietly read through the summary, scanned the reviews, and gazed through its contents. After making a small noise of doubt, I set the book aside on the table behind me with three others and hunted for another.

"Are you almost finished?" Crystal blurted. She sat at the opposite end of a table, setting her watchful gaze on me with her chin propped in her hand. I could hear the blasting music from her earphones from where I was.

"What? I thought you liked novels."

"I already found mine, but you're taking way too long."

I had already finished all the novels I had back at home and read them over twice. After finding some time to get away from my dad, I made a trip to Barnes & Noble, taking Crystal with me. Since I was rarely allowed to go the bookstore anymore, it was crucial to buy as many as I could now.

I checked the time on my watch, realizing only then that I had been here for nearly an hour. "I might be here just a bit longer. Why don't you go check out the music section?" With a flick of my head, I gestured to the glass-concealed room on the upper floor.

After taking a moment for what I had just said to sink in, Crystal leaped up from her chair and ran to the music section, her light brown hair swishing behind her as she carried her books with her.

Before I could turn back to the shelves to find something else, something struck me. Skillet had just released a new album! I picked up my books and held them against my chest as I ran after Crystal.

Winter had just begun in California. It had been five months since Jared had dropped me off at home after our time in LA. Since then, he periodically scanned the perimeter around me to make sure Carlos wasn't following me. Jared said that Carlos would want revenge twice as badly now that Jared had turned the government's attention toward him.

I'd been trying my hardest to retain a normal life, despite my dad, starting by sneaking out of the house and hanging out with Crystal.

Once I managed to catch up with Crystal, I found my way around the shelves of CDs to the *S* section, picked up Skillet's album, and turned the case around to check the price.

"I didn't know you were a book person," a familiar voice marveled behind me.

I swung around to find Jared leaning against a tall shelf of dubstep CDs. I held his gaze—a warm smile with eyes that moved with serenity.

"What are you doing here?" I asked, surprised at his sudden appearance. I began to wonder if Jared had spotted Carlos somewhere nearby. My eyes moved to the windows before scanning the bookstore. "Is he—?"

Jared shook his head. "Haven't seen him in a week." In one swift movement, he was standing before me. "But that's not stopping me from seeing my Cupid." I could feel his warmth caressing my skin. His minty breath combined with his natural scent of earth and herbs made me break into a smile.

Jared set his gaze on the books and CD in my arms. "Here, I'll get you these for free." He reached for the products, but I swung them out of his reach.

"You are *not* deceiving the cashier like last time." Undesirable memories of Jared's deceiving came roaring back to me. At first, I thought it was pretty cool that he could trick people into letting him buy free things.

Now I didn't want that.

The first time, it was completely necessary—we needed to stay somewhere that was the last place the government would look. But doing it every day made me a criminal.

"Let me pay. I've been saving," I added, trying to walk past him.

Jared held me back. "All right, Cupid. But take this." He stuffed a ten-dollar bill into my right jeans pocket.

Before I could open my mouth to protest, Crystal's voice sang from the other side of the tall shelf we were at. "Hey, Destiny, check out this album from Seether." She rounded the shelf corner and met up with me.

When I turned back around to face Jared, he was gone.

"Look, look. It comes with all the songs on the deluxe edition." Crystal pointed at several songs on the list.

I had the feeling that whatever we thought we'd left behind wasn't over. Carlos was bouncing right back for revenge, and here I was—here *Jared* was—risking everything to try to live in peace. Again.

We'd paid for everything, and I had kept Jared's money to get something to eat. I didn't have any food at home for the weekend, and I had my dad and his obsession with beer to thank for that.

After we slumped in the car and started the engine, I shifted through everything in my Barnes & Noble bag. "Is it just me, or do you love that awesome smell of new books?" I opened up one of the novels and brought it to my nose, inhaling the scent of fresh paper and vanilla coffee. "They should have a perfume for this."

"Agreed. Let's send Victoria's Secret an e-mail request."

"I would so buy one—two." I smiled as I cranked up the heat, pushing out the cold air that rushed in from outside. It always snowed closer to where I lived, since my house was far from the warmth of city life. If I was lucky, I would encounter light sprinkles of small snowflakes, falling to the earth like white feathers in the middle of an outside shopping square.

I popped open Skillet's album and slid the disk into the CD player, rolling the windows down to let others hear the music as we peeled out of the parking lot and out to the open road.

THE ROOM AROUND CARLOS LAW seemed to darken as he ripped out a handful of black feathers from Jared's wings, which were now fused to his back. Igniting a flame, his match clicked to life as he held the feathers over the ember, burning them. The black bristles shook before they shriveled and deteriorated.

But it was no use. The feathers just rematerialized back into the wings.

The one person he hated—and now he was stuck with his wings as a part of his body. The smell of the burning feathers barely fed the fiery hunger of his anger.

I'm going to find you, Jared, he thought. *And I swear to god, I* will *kill you.* He knew the meaning behind the words was dead. He couldn't kill an immortal, but there had to be another way.

He curled his hand into a fist and then loosened it, watching the dust and ashes fall from his cold palm.

But I'll keep your wings—for now. You've given me an advantage over you. He spoke as if Jared was right next to him.

As if signaled, Carlo's lips curved upward in a dark, cynical smile. The plot had worked its way into his brain so fast, so effortlessly, he couldn't help but apprehend it.

I'll use that pretty girlfriend of yours when she's not realizing it. You won't be prepared for what is to come.

ACKNOWLEDGMENTS

I have so many people to thank. I'll try my best to add everyone.

Crestfallen would never have happened if not for the awesome team at Simon & Schuster and their enthusiasm for helping me publish my book! AI, for helping me with writing ever since my beginnings in fan fiction and motivating me to publish *Crestfallen*; Yelena, for being my first fan girl and reading the first steps of the *Crestfallen* project; and all who read and reviewed *Solitude* on Fictionpress—I can't thank you guys enough.

Also, I'd like to offer a very unique thanks to Mr. Drinks for that "unintentional writing project" that got me started with writing! (Do I still get a grade for it?)

I'm grateful as well for my family's support and eagerness for me to write and publish.

Finally, I thank Gaelle Augustine for always inspiring my ideas, beginning on that day in art class when we literally took out a piece of paper and started jotting down ideas.

ABOUT THE AUTHOR

Gabriella Francis began writing her first novel, *Crestfallen,* when she was fourteen. After sharing it on Fictionpress, she received positive feedback and decided to officially publish it. Gabriella lives in Miami, Florida, where she enjoys listening to rock music, watching Anime, reading, drawing, and of course, writing.